SEA MUSIC

SEA MUSIC

David Profumo

SECKER & WARBURG
L O N D O N

First published in England 1988 by
Martin Secker & Warburg Limited
54 Poland Street, London W1V 3DF

Copyright © 1988 by David Profumo

Reprinted 1988

British Library Cataloguing in Publication Data
Profumo, David
Sea music
I. Title
823'.914[F]   PR6066.R6/

ISBN 0-436-38714-X

The extract from *Wolves* is reprinted by
permission of Faber and Faber Ltd
from *Collected Poems* by Louis MacNeice.

Printed and bound in Great Britain
by Billing & Sons Limited, Worcester.

For Helen, James and Tom

'I want to know what it says,' he answered, looking steadily in her face. 'The sea, Floy, what is it that it keeps saying?'
  She told him that it was only the noise of the rolling waves.

Charles Dickens, from *Dombey and Son*, (1848)

'Come then all of you, come closer, form a circle,
Join hands and make believe that joined
Hands will keep away the wolves of water
Who howl along our coast. And be it assumed
That no-one hears them among the talk and laughter . . .'

Louis MacNeice, from *Wolves*, (1934)

I

A thorn of light entered the room from the passage outside.
The dormitory was a wash of muffled sounds, the boys whispering while the prefect was out. Brass-bound trunks were
stacked in the centre of the room, conjured from the depths
of the school buildings, their reappearance the embodiment of
eager weeks of wishing. There was nothing else in the world
that seemed to matter, except departure.

'We're going to fly there,' said one voice, 'and stay for a
whole month. It's going to be brilliant.'

'I'm off to Italy.'

'Dugdale . . . typical!'

'What about you, Benson?' asked the boy in the bed next
to him. James Benson had his face to the door; he was staring
out along the corridor with its shiny walls of cream and dark
green paint.

'Benson. Hey, Benson. Where are you off to – for hols?'

'An island,' the pale boy replied, without turning. 'With
my father. He's taking me to an island.'

'Gosh. A hot one, with swimming?'

He gave a small shrug under the sheets. 'I don't know. I
don't think so.'

The chatter ebbed as the prefect returned, the door closed,
and the borrowed light was shut out. Excitement had exhausted most of them, and soon the noise of breathing was all
that remained in the dark. The July night was hunched and
hot outside, with the blurred sound of distant traffic. Like the
others, James drifted to sleep, but later he surfaced suddenly
from the rhythm of his dream and felt himself the only one
awake in the large room.

Through the curtains, wide open against the gathered heat,

he could see above the trees a shape of the night sky, which had taken on the colours of blue where the bright moon showed like a flake of pebble below water. There was even an owl somewhere out there, it must have been on the fringes of the playing-fields, its low enquiring sounds floating through the night.

The boy turned away from the window, his eyes towards the closed door. Flickering anticipation made him rehearse each detail of the coming day's release. It was part of the ritual. He prayed to himself that his father would not be too late in arriving; to watch through the smeary panes of a library window as the rest of the school drained eagerly away was a depressing start to the holidays. He sometimes had a dream that he was the only person left inside the shell of the school's building, and even the teachers had packed up and gone. But still there was no sign of the car, and no exciting scrunch of gravel as it swept past the rhododendrons and glided up to the door. Tomorrow, though, it would be different. He would be one of the first to be collected, and the others would look at his father's new car, and the two of them would speed away together, and Slatebrook School would be behind them, with all its dark furniture, the ringing corridors and hollow-sounding floors which sent up puffs of dust.

James smiled. His eyes were now closed, and he thought of the owl in its clear inches of moonlight. Once more he was sleeping.

II

'I'll say one thing for this place of yours,' announced Michael Cooper, 'the water's so soft you can hardly wash the soap off your face.'

James's father looked up from the breakfast table. 'I see you managed to cut yourself to shreds all the same. You should get yourself one of these electric ones from America.' The man's throat had two smudges of blood on it, and he laughed. 'Not much good to you up here if the generator packs up.' He rubbed his hands together histrionically and approached the hot plate, where three dishes were covered with battered metal cloches.

Richard Benson shovelled some crumbly egg on to his toast. He pursed his lips. 'Egg's powdered, too,' he said. 'You'd think with all those hens running around that a proper egg was a possibility.'

'Using up the rations, I expect.'

The air was tinged with sandalwood as the man took his place next to James, who was sipping tea and gazing out of the window at the bay, its surface webbed with light.

'Any papers?' asked Michael. A lick of his dark, oiled hair slid forward as he bent over his plate. Richard snorted at him without looking up; he was reading through some records in a wide ledger bound in pigskin. 'On the Sabbath? You must be joking. Nothing around here moves on the Sabbath, except the long line of penitents to church. Nothing else allowed.'

Even at school, James thought, you could have sweets and play games on Sunday. It was the best day of the whole week.

'Soon be the same back home, if they get their way,' said Michael. 'Lord's Day Observance Society – telling the Duke he can't play polo on Sundays. I don't know. Got offices in Fleet Street, I hear.' He was a few years older than Richard, and his manner was militaristic, though his figure had filled out since leaving the Army. A large paisley-patterned hand-kerchief spilled from the top pocket of his blazer. There was a slim line of whiskers running along the top of his cheek.

It had taken them two days of travel to reach the lodge. The three cars had driven north in convoy together, through Glasgow and as far as Fort William; they had then separated to catch different ferries. The boy was intrigued by the strangeness of the landscape through which they passed, the patchy crops yellowing in the drought, the moorland umber and shimmering, with only the odd purple splash of bell-heather. The lochs and rivers were shrivelled and showing their stones. He had never been to Scotland before; he had not realised how far away it was from the places he thought of as the centre of the country, from Surrey and from school. In Geography, they had always looked at it on a separate map.

His father had been irritable because the heat wave meant the fishing would be poor. James listened dutifully as he com-plained in advance about the sport, and the cost, and the dis-tance, but he himself was not disappointed, for he shared none of his father's passions. He was pleased to be going somewhere new, to a place none of the party had ever visited before. At one stage they had lost their way, and Benson had asked why he had to have a son so incapable of reading a simple map. On Skye, the car was winched on to the ferry in a sling. The *Loch Mor* only had a tiny car deck, and the others had not been able to book a berth; they were taking the longer route from Mallaig. The difficulties of getting there were to James part of the fun; to his father they were evidence of admini-strative inefficiency.

They had made the crossing on a fine August evening, the greys of the seascape tilting a broken light. The boy watched the wake of the steamer unpeel and collapse behind it. Satellite gulls billowed and creaked around the stern of the black and red vessel, lunging up into its slipstream for the bread he hurled to them. At his first sight of the jagged island ahead, he had run in to tell his father who was reading in the dining area, his documents stacked out next to the wreckage of his supper, a rind of meat pie and a pattern of damp peas.

'We're almost there,' the boy had informed him eagerly.

The ship was approaching a barren-looking headland that formed one arm of the harbour. Richard looked but said nothing. A whirl of cigar smoke came out of his mouth.

The wash from the propellers ran in a curl along the shore, lifting a thick tangle of kelp and sea-ware in its swell, but above the tide-line there was little growing. The puckered rock formation was spiky with thin sea-grass and there was scarcely any soil. In the distance, two speckled hills curved against the lemon evening sky; there were white patches on their slopes, some of which were sheep, and some were further outcrops of pale gneiss bulging up through the moorland. The boy craned over the handrail, his fair hair blowing like flames.

By the time they had arrived at the pier, his father had joined him on deck, his attaché case under one arm. He looked disapproving as he surveyed the little township, its scatter of houses an alien arrangement to his orderly southern eye. The ferry bumped perfectly against the pier-head, the reverse thrust of its screws churning brain-like shapes in the water.

The dark-green sports saloon had been lowered to the dock. They moved off up the main street, and at the top they swung north. The road soon deteriorated badly; it was potholed every few yards, and Benson had to change gear constantly, steering an unsteady progress along the bitten coast. Even more than the mainland hills they had left behind, the massive contours of these new surroundings surprised the boy, but their bareness seemed welcoming. It was a clean, uncluttered vista. Between the road and the sea an occasional low white house was clamped to the shoreline, but to their right, where the foothills began to rise away, there was a moonscape of boulders and scree. There was not a tree to be seen on the wind-cleared faces of the rock where shorn sheep, their skins daubed with dye, hobbled in search of vegetation.

The streamlined Healey with its fuming driver had plunged its way towards the hills.

. . . . .

The north side of the little graveyard was the only area not planted out with headstones, but near the drystone wall there was one mound, and here she bent, and placed the yellow flowers, iris and dandelion. Here alone, in this island without the cover of trees, among people with no locked doors, there was physical privacy. As she stooped below the shelter of the wall, even the current of the wind was excluded. The ground was badged with moss, and rose-bay willow-herb flickered over tiny orchids. Here at least was rich ground. She laid one hand on the hump of grassy soil, as if to feel a ripeness. It was not a place of sadness any more, as she stared directly at the ground, her voice a soft whirr.

'*Mo Chubhrachan.*' My fragrant one.

The woman turned as a large green car drove past into the evening.

III

In front of Graeval Lodge was a narrow lawn stapled with rusting hoops, and beyond that a long sloping beach of shingle. The boy walked out around the building and began to make his way up the slope behind, clambering over the creased rocks with their velvety mapwork of lichen. He did not have to climb far before he could see across the bay to his right, with the little river threading down the headland into it. He saw a couple of fish bounce out of the water, and then something darker made a swirl just under the surface, but it was too far to tell what it might be.

The hillside was flowery with sunlight and the long dry scent of the heather above. He realised he should have put on his boots, for even in the prolonged heat there were soggy yellow expanses between the rocks, and their fibrous liquid seeped through the vents of his sandals. James did not feel like losing sight of the lodge itself, so he worked his way along the slope and around the bay without climbing higher into the folds of the hill. There was somewhere above him the noise of larks singing down into the morning, invisibly high.

He managed to cross the little river without getting any wetter, for its current had so dwindled it scarcely made a curl as it went into the sea. At the far side of the bay, he looked back at the dilapidated white lodge towering on its promontory, its regular lines and slender arrangements of chimneys at variance with the stony swirls of the landscape where it stood planted, by the calm movements of the level sea. There was nobody to be seen, except, smudged with heat out towards the horizon, the twin bones of a yacht under sail.

When he rounded the point, the shoreline of rocks and greasy weed soon gave way to a short beach of whitish shells and, and beyond that a series of dunes. The tide was out, and the sand was printed with ripple. James took off his shoes and socks, and rolled up his grey flannel trousers. He ran out along the strand and stood, feeling his toes being absorbed into the sinking mass of wet sand. It sucked and simmered around his feet.

'Lava,' he said, aloud. 'I'm a volcano.' He shuffled along parallel to the water, raising twin ridges of the stuff as he ploughed it with arched toes. He was happy being on his own. One of the things he disliked most about living at school was the constant pressure of doing everything in the company of others. You were always in a team or group, a queue or a class, and they wouldn't leave you to your own devices. Even during the afternoon rest, you had to be reading a book, and were not allowed to close your eyes. It seemed silly. You saw things when your eyes were closed, and sometimes that was the only way you could think clearly. People never left you alone. James enjoyed his holidays because, on the whole, he did not mind if he was ignored.

A small white bird with pointed wings was chasing a gull through the sky. After one swerve, the gull discharged from its beak a thin stream of silvery eels which the other bird inhaled as they fell, before swooping away over the water. They disappeared against the sky, shrieking at each other. He turned and made his way back towards the lodge.

One side of the courtyard behind Graeval was a long room, its doors and window-frames painted the estate's uniform blue, and as James passed it he heard voices, and he looked in. His father and the other men were standing around a large central table which was heaped with items of tackle. They were fingering flies out of boxes, twirling the ratchets of reels, and giving each other advice. There was a glass-fronted cabinet at the far end, massive and stocked with guns in vertical racks, while parallel along the walls ranged horizontal lines of assorted rods. The air was smoky and damp, sharp with whisky.

'Well, it's the intrepid explorer himself,' said a portly, grey-faced man. Dr Willis came from the West Country, and smelled of violets. He was perpetually jovial in a tense sort of way, and usually greeted the boy with a rumpling of the hair, which James found annoying. His father had known him since the war. 'Checked out the lie of the land, have we?' The boy said he had seen some fish in the bay.

He went into the lodge to get ready for lunch. The building did not feel strange to him, because its huge rooms and uncomfortable beds reminded him of school; they had the same cavernous baths and the paint on the walls was dull, and blistered with damp. His bedroom was on the second floor and had been a servant's room before the war, when Graeval was a family home. From the window there was no view of the sea, only the yard and the rising mass of the mountain itself. He filled the basin with cold, hazel-coloured water, and plopped in a new cake of soap, watching it uncoil its filmy white ribbons. From outside he could hear the laughter of the men leaving the tackle room, and beyond that the faint breathing of the ocean. It was distant but distinct, like the soft memory of a colour preserved in dried flowers.

.   .   .   .   .

'Campbell, I want you to keep an eye on my son James,' his father instructed the under-keeper the next morning.

'Very good,' replied Alec Campbell. 'But Grant has told me to clean the vehicles. Every Monday morning, sir, that is to be the arrangement.'

Richard was climbing into some waders. He made an impatient gesture with one hand: 'Well, the boy can help you. Bring him up to the hut for lunch.'

'Right,' said Alec, 'I will.'

They watched the rest of the party climb into the Land Rover, stowing their rods and tackle with meticulous care. Dr Willis gave James a wave, and stretched his arms suddenly as if measuring a fish. They moved off. The boy turned to look at his companion. He was a severe-looking islander with sandy-coloured hair and wiry eyebrows that twisted off his forehead like spray. He was wearing a checked shirt and tweed breeches, with thick white woollen socks. His face and peeling forearms were already varnished with sweat.

'Will they catch anything, do you think?' asked James. Alec gave a laugh like the cough of pebbles into a well. He looked sideways at the boy.

'If I could tell that, I'd be a rich man. But I'm thinking we're better off here where we are. There's scarcely a fish in the loch. They're out in the bay, there, man. Waiting for the water. They'll not run the river without it.' Alec made his way across the yard in search of buckets and cloths. He walked jaggedly, with a limp.

They were standing in front of a small black car. 'Have you met the Beast?' enquired Alec, the blues gleaming in his eyes. The boy was not sure what to say. 'Well, we call yon fellow the Beast because one time, when he was the only vehicle to be had, I brought back a beast on his roof.' James stared at the car in bewilderment.

The man smiled. 'Deer, boy. A beast from the brae there. Graeval.' He filled two buckets with brown water.

'Is that where they live, on the top?'

'Right on the very top, I'm telling you. And a long way down it is if you've a beast or two to pull along with you.'

'Can we go up there one day?'

Alec slapped his sponge on to the roof of the Standard and squeezed it. He watched the water run over the rim and down the glass. 'Not even Sherpa Tenzing could get there with my leg,' he said, starting to rub the paintwork.

'Why, what's happened?' As he spoke, he wondered if he was being rude.

'Ach, a small accident in the desert,' said the man. 'I drove my cycle into a shell-hole. In November of nineteen-forty-two, during the artillery fire.' He clacked his tongue twice. 'Broke it clean; two places. So it's no more high ground for me; and this fellow,' he said tapping the brightwork of the mirror, 'will never be carting a beast any more. That's all changed, right enough. I'm with the kennels now, and the boats and the like.'

'My father was in the desert,' said James. 'He was a Captain, and got a medal.'

'Well. Is that so?' said the islander neutrally. He began to polish a headlamp. 'That's a fine thing to have. A medal.'

. . . . .

'And is that right – that you've never seen a lobster?' said Alec in his slow voice, as the Beast squealed out of the yard and into the arena of the afternoon sun. 'Well, they're here in plenty when you know where to find them. It will be a sore thing for Donald Angus if he has not one or two to show us, the day.' The interior of the little Standard reeled with his cigarette smoke.

Three miles down the single-track road, Alec forked left and there was a narrow causeway reaching across the estuary, the sea running in with the afternoon tide. At the end of the road there was a wooden hut and a short stone jetty stacked with wickerwork creels and the bright globes of buoys; a twenty-foot boat, without a wheel-house, shrugged up and down on the swell, its engine still beating.

'Well. She's back, at any rate.' Alec swung his leg unhurriedly out of the car and tilted his cap on to the back of his head.

'Hulloo there.' A grey-haired man straightened up from the hollow of the hull, an arm stretched in greeting. He held a dark, flapping crustacean in each hand.

'Twelve,' he said to Alec, as they stepped on to the jetty. It was hard to tell from his smile whether he was pleased or merely joking. 'And two with the berries on, that are gone back.' He nodded at the boy.

'You're sure now. And no scraping?' Alec sounded as if he were treating the older man like a child. 'He's a devil for scraping the eggs off yon females, and pretending they are clean for the market, the wee fellow,' he said to James.

Donald Angus stood over six foot high in the frisking boat, the lobsters still in his grasp. The sky above him was littered with gulls.

'We'd better be seeing them, Donald.' James was lifted down into the boat by his armpits, and stood looking at the creatures crouched in the wooden fish-box. They had inky, arched backs, and he was frightened they might suddenly spring, like insects. A soft rustling sound came from the crate. The claws were tied closed with rubber bands, and lay like clubs in front of the sharp heads, two slow aerials of antennae tapering up over them, feeling the useless air.

'I thought they were red,' said the boy. They made him uneasy.

'And so they will be, right enough. Soon as they're away to London and over to the Frenchies that want them. They'll boil up red, and no mistake – all except this boy.' Alec rapped on the shell of the largest, and one of the eyes jerked on its stalk. The back of the lobster was cratered with broken barnacles. 'They'll no take them that big, nothing over the pound-and-a-half. He'd maybe do for the lodge, though. We'll keep him back for Kirsty.'

He lifted it from the box, the tail clacking and the frilly white undercarriage shuffling in mid-air, and lowered it gently into a broad-bottomed bucket. James did not much care for the idea of sharing a car-ride with this menacingly limbed creature, but he said nothing. He did not want Alec to think badly of him.

The car quivered and started, and Alec peeped the horn twice, waving to the man on the jetty. They crept back up the track.

'The Colonel here,' said Alec, jerking a thumb towards the pail on the back seat, 'is one of your swiftest swimmers in the ocean, along with the seal and the salmon. But there's like to be one more swim in him only, and that's in Kirsty's fish kettle. She makes a tasty sauce, so I'm told, if there's the butter to be had.'

James was quiet, staring through the open window at the long curve of water going out to the horizon. He wished he had not gone with Alec to see the lobsters. From books, he had always imagined them to be silent animals, picking their way across a muffled gloom of sand in a slow crawl; but now he realised that in their own element they were quick, and he knew their noises, down to the faint tapping of trussed claws sliding around the smooth tin of a bucket. And, when you cooked them, Alec said, they screamed.

They clattered over the wooden planking of a bridge, and the car pulled up in a passing-place. 'Now. We'll just take a look at the river,' said Alec, rubbing the bristly back of his neck. 'As if we didn't know it would be hopeless.' They made their way down the bank, peering into the bouldery little pools through which a low stream was crawling its way. 'That's where we need the water-level,' said the man, pointing to a spot more than half-way up the dry bank, where there was a fringe of bony flotsam cast by the spring floods. He spat into the pool. 'Not a chance of a fish making it up in this: he'd have his head out of the water. What a summer, for God's sake.'

At the mouth of the little river, where James had crossed that morning with the tide out, the shoals of salmon had now moved inshore, and in places the water was thorny with dorsal fins swinging together above the feeble current. 'Hungry for rain,' Alec said, pointing instinctively as each leaping fish shivered out of the sea.

'Is that why they jump?' asked James.

'That, or there's maybe something after them. In the ocean, you can't rightly tell.'

The man suddenly crouched down, his bad leg out at an awkward angle. He pointed at a patch of thin grass that was scorched. 'Otters.' Alec was hissing. He passed a hand over the ground as if to feel an actual heat. He rubbed a finger and thumb under his nose. 'Dog otter,' he said. 'Spraying his patch, so he is. He'll take dozens of them, the bastard. If you're seeing what I mean.'

James looked at him, and by way of explanation the man suddenly clutched a fold of skin at the nape of his neck, and wrenched it slightly. 'That's all he'll take, a single bite. And that's an end on it.' Alec straightened up slowly, and turned away from the water. 'Christ, man, with this weather. There's only one thing for it.'

Another salmon smacked back into the tide, and he rolled his eyes without even bothering to look. 'Otters,' explained Alec, 'is the least of our worries.'

Taller than any other vegetation to be seen, a thick bed of irises rose from the far bank, the yellow flowers now crumpled and blown. 'Did you ever make a dream boat?' asked Alec, nodding towards the stems. They jumped across on the stones, and he began twisting together some of the long green leaves. 'Now when I was your age – no, I was younger, a wee boy maybe – my father used to make them for me.' He began to fold and plait the stringy foliage into the shape of a crude little raft. His broad hands were oddly neat in their movements, and the fingers had a delicacy and a sureness as they looped and tied the object together.

Alec placed it on the boy's outstretched palm. 'Well?' he challenged him. James told him politely that it was very nice, and he would keep it carefully. 'That's never for keeping, man,' said Alec, feigning exasperation. 'Away with you now and launch it on to the sea, and don't forget to whisper your wish, or that dream of yours will never come true, not even when the boat is found again by another person.'

The man watched him approach the shore obediently and launch the boat where the fresh water pushed out into the sea. It spun around slowly for a few moments and then floated away from the land, above the ranks of waiting fish, over the bluish feathers of their bodies, the dark metal of their backs. James stared until it seemed to disappear, but he did not make a wish.

IV

His attention swung between one wave of conversation and
another, as the men talked busily under a mass of cigar smoke.
James was not bored by the discussions, but enjoyed a comfortable distance from what was being said, realising he was
not expected to understand very much of it. Since the two
women had retired upstairs to the drawing-room, no one had
addressed a remark directly to him, but he caught occasional
snatches of the spoken shapes, like glimpses through the
louvres of a blind. Through the quick murmur of opinions,
the boy's gaze drifted to the window, where the water beyond
was weaving in the evening light. Individual voices rose and
plunged: he followed the rhythm of their sounds, and felt
quite happy, comfortable on the fringes of the adults'
evening.

Turning to his neighbour, Richard Benson raised his pitch
and said, 'You're an Oxford man, Michael. What would you
say was the single most important piece of advice you were
ever offered as a student?' There was something artificial in
his tone which quelled the talking of the others. Cooper
blustered and cupped his chin; his partner was well known
for cutting across the grain. He shook his head helplessly at
the *non sequitur*.

'Well, don't cudgel your brains about it. I'll tell you mine.
My tutor at London, Johnny Garrett – dead now, poor chap
– instilled in me this most valuable maxim: a proper gentleman never lets the port stick at his elbow.' Michael Cooper's
eyes dropped instinctively to his right, and there came from
the others a rustle of laughter. 'Not me,' he replied.

James unravelled his gaze from the window. He realised
they were now all staring at him.

'The port,' intoned Benson. 'I am asking you, young man, to push the boat out.' He was not smiling, and the boy peered flatly at him, lost.

Bobby Paton leaned across and stage-whispered into his ear, 'Pass on the decanter, if you're finished with it.' The port, in its ridiculous wheeled cradle, had come to rest by the boy's tumbler of lemonade.

'If you are going to stay up with us like this, you will have to learn the rules of the mess,' said his father, his face folded with disapproval. James's embarrassment went down under a discharge of laughter.

Raising his glass in the fork of two slim fingers, Paton seemed to address his observations to the fat, gleaming wine as the discussion resumed in a rumble of noise. 'This much I do know,' he said in his faint drawl; 'since the Tories took the helm, shall we say, the fur trade has rocketed. Boom isn't the word to describe it. This year at auction we've grossed more than double any pre-war figure already, and that's just our end of it. Good God: if people in the know are buying furs, they'll grab anything.'

He looked up challengingly from his twirled glass, where legs of liquid were converging towards the stem.

'It's beginning to happen,' continued Paton thinly. '"Set the People Free," that was Churchill's challenge, and, let's face it, he meant the freedom of choice. The basic, the decent freedom to spend their hard-earned money across the country the way that they choose, without those artificial constraints, those clamps of a Labour economy.'

Michael Cooper was shifting in his chair. 'Vermin, they called us. But who's pulled the country round, that's what I ask. Unit Trusts, Lloyds – cocoa, wool. Some vermin we turned out to be!' He bellowed smoke triumphantly at the candles.

'Well, Bevan got his backside kicked for that.'

'If Fox-Strangways hadn't booted him out of White's, then I would have done so for him.'

'It would need a long reach from Boodle's.'

'None the less.'

James's father began clearing a sightline through the crockery and glass; he leant forward in Bobby Paton's direction and aimed a finger at him disarmingly. 'So that's what we all fought for, Bobby, is it? The freedom to buy furs?'

'You sound like Gilbert Harding.'

'I'm glad. But I mean it. The trouble is, you're not looking far enough ahead. The people who are snapping up your luxuries today are the ones who are going to need what I'm building tomorrow. It's a question of long-term growth, not the easy foam off the mixture. We've got one-hundred-per cent employment, and a government committed to the whole idea of national wealth. It's not just that austerity is out – so is nostalgia. That's what's kept us all down, the memory of the good old days. When people wore fur. The affluence of the future, that's what interests me – a different deck of cards altogether. When people want things they don't even know that they want. That's where we come in.' He glanced reassuringly at Cooper.

'Oh, I see. Benson Cooper will be building houses that people don't think they want. Priceless!'

Benson was in his element. He leant back and swept his eyes to the ceiling. 'Not at all. Creating a demand, that's what I'm saying. There's a shortage of housing *now*, of course there is, but you can't think in terms of immediate needs. Restrictions are off: I'm looking to the end of the decade. Where people live now is no concern of mine – let the councils sort that out; that's what they like doing anyway – I'm going to build houses for this country to grow into.'

'Should we join the ladies, do you think?' ventured Dr Willis. He placed his hands on the table to announce that he wished to rise. The men hauled themselves up in a scraping of chairs.

'"I've fought my war," I told my foreman in Crawley,

"but now I'm going to make my real killing."'' Benson nodded once at his own observation, and Bobby Paton demuringly raised both hands towards him, as if offering a tray, or surrendering a sword. They had heard it before, but that didn't matter. It was good, fighting talk all the same, the stuff of the future. They were all in it together.

James helped his father snuff the candles, blowing sharply around his thumb, so the wax would not spatter. 'Nip through and let Kirsty know we're finished?' The boy nodded.

'Aha,' said Dr Willis, one foot heavily on the bottom stair, 'popping off to inspect my triumph, I suppose?' James stopped, his elbow against the swing-door leading to the kitchen, and looked round.

'Sorry?'

'Stealing a peek at my finnock, eh?' The doctor raised a finger to his eye. 'Come on, then, and I'll show you.' They went down the paved passageway together and stopped at the slab where, under a sprinkler of fine water, were displayed the crispy, freckled bodies of three small fish on a slab.

'Little sparklers, aren't they?'

James looked at the corpses; their eyes had gone milky, and the membranes were wrinkled and soft. 'What are they – little salmon?' He was more polite than curious.

'Wish they had been. No, no, alas. Finnock. Young sea-trout. But we must be grateful for small mercies.'

'They don't look very big.' He realised he was sounding rude.

'Just the ticket for breakfast, though, with bacon, if there is any.'

'Did you catch them in the sea?'

'No, not a chance. In the loch up there – caught them all myself, I did; top rod. All three!'

The boy feigned admiration. He did not say that he had seen much larger fish jumping in the estuary, because the man was already looking crestfallen. 'Didn't my father catch anything?'

'Afraid not. But you know him. He will. Early days yet.'

'Yes,' he said, 'yes.'

Dr Willis steered him up the stairs, a hand on his shoulder.

'Come and sit next to me, James dear,' said Rosemary Cooper. She accompanied the invitation with a pat-pat of the sofa cushion, peering round-eyed from her circle of light. She waved at him with her sampler. 'Did you have fun today? I hope so. Did you explore?'

Her bones looked hollow and thin, her face like a bird's. She cocked her head graciously as he sat down. The boy told her about the boat and the lobsters.

'Poor little things,' she agreed, 'but so delicious.'

'What's he like, that Campbell fellow?' asked her husband, settling himself opposite them, by the gloomy fireplace. 'Look after you all right?'

James nodded eagerly. 'He has a car called the Beast. We had fun.'

Cooper rattled his cup. 'Beats me how he can drive at all. I mean, the poor man's been crippled. Could be dangerous in a tight spot on the road.'

'I'm sure he knows what he's doing,' said Rosemary, one hand feeling the pearls at her throat. 'He looks most capable. And traffic doesn't seem to be much of a problem up here, does it?'

'All the same. Not my idea of an able-bodied keeper. Grant doesn't think so either.'

'It happened in the war.' James surprised himself by interrupting. 'In the desert; he had an accident.' He looked at one and then the other.

'I told you.' Cooper flipped up his spoon triumphantly.

'Who would have imagined,' enquired his wife, squinting along her embroidery scissors, 'that all the way up here in the wilds one would come across a man who was wounded in the desert?'

'It was an accident, not a wound,' said Cooper.

'He walks all right,' James added. 'There's nothing wrong with him.'

'Well, whatever. Poor man.' Tidily, she snipped off the wool.

James slid off the sofa and crossed the room to the table where, by a wall spiky with antlers, his father was now dealing cards.

'Off to Bedfordshire?' asked Dr Willis. 'Not such a bad idea at that.' He dragged a fobwatch from the piped pocket of his smoking jacket, and clicked his tongue automatically, as if in sympathy with its mechanism. He offered his hand to the boy. 'Sleep tight.'

He said goodnight to his father; he raised his hand to the others.

'Are you sure you're all right, up there in that room of yours?' asked Rosemary, engulfing his head in her shawled arms. She kissed his hair gently. James left the tall green room, its atmosphere thick as smog; he closed the heavy door on the clatter of talk, and the soft soapy smell of Rosemary Cooper's cashmere wings.

Upstairs, he clambered into his striped flannel pyjamas and lay in the envelope of faintly damp sheets. Through the window, reflected from the rocks of the hillside, there came the thick sound of water gathering on to the shore. He tried to imagine where his iris boat might be, turning and twindling out in the near dark, but he still would not wish. His father had told him, after all, that it would be hopeless, and in his mind the whole thing was sealed off. They would not be seeing her any more.

Dark blue sky arced, a shell starred with barnacles.

V

He held the slice in his thick hand; it looked like a hunk of continental bread. Alec crumbled off a brown grain with his thumb; there was the white vein of a root in it.

'It's maybe not the best, but it's what we have. We'll no get the fine white ash when this lot goes into the ribs of the fire, but there'll be heat, and that's the first thing.' He flipped the peat into the sack which the boy held open beside him.

The man was dressed in dungarees, not the tweed uniform that he had to wear when on duty. James watched the sweat spawning on his neck as he leant once again to the pile, grunting as he clattered the peats into the sack.

The cut oblongs of earth were surprisingly regular, propped along the top of the bog in groups of four. James and Alec stood in the trench and leaned against the dark wall of the hillside; the vertical surface from which the peats had been scooped was almost smooth, so precise was the sweep of the crofters' blades. It looked like a pattern of tiles.

Two sacks were stuffed to the brim, and one other was half filled.

'You'll not be wanting to manage more than that for the first time down,' said Alec, settling himself on the bulging hessian. He pulled a brown beer-bottle from his pocket and clicked the top off with his knife. 'And there's four trips to make to the Beast, if my Auntie Rachel is to have sufficient for her fire.'

It was three days before the start of the shooting season, and Willie Grant had given him the day off to lift his peats from the hill, the last opportunity he would have until the guests left the lodge. Alec finished his drink and drove the bottle neck-first into the ground with the heel of his boot. It disappeared half-way, and there was a soft grinding sound.

'We'll be needing a new cutting come May,' he said gloomily, looking down at the brown bulb of glass. 'That's down to the clay now.'

He pointed to several bare stretches down towards the road, where the peat had been stripped from the hill. 'When it's worked out, you've the skinned land – *gearraidh*. Gone for good, up in smoke. Next year, you have to move on. Or up.'

'There's a big basket of peat in the drawing-room,' said James, 'but we haven't had a fire yet. Nobody's lit one.'

'And who'd be wanting it, with this weather?' Alec jerked a thumb at the sky. 'Besides, we're awful modern in the island, now. We've the coal to burn, too. But you try to tell that to my Auntie – she'll use nothing but the peats for her cooking, and she's always minding that winter will be around the corner of the year before we know it. Thousands of the things, she burns, and no mistake, boy.'

They laughed together, for the first time, squatting in the angle of the hill.

'They're like bricks,' said James. 'You could build a house with them.'

Alec nodded. 'Bricks of peat, that's what they are. It's the wind makes them hard.'

'Isn't there somewhere closer? I mean; it's a long way to carry them to the road.'

In reply, Alec hoisted him on to the top of the cutting, and faced him up the hill. 'You mark what looks to be a pile of old stones on yon ridge there?' James nodded. 'In my grandfather's time, now, that was the summer shielings, and it's here that we have the rights to the peat, as a consequence. Never mind they're mine now, the places for cutting stay the same. All over the island.'

The boy stared at the distant tumble of stones where people had once lived: the buildings had been deliberately flattened, the walls dragged apart, a jawbone's wreckage.

'It was the cattle that needed it,' the man continued, rubbing dampness from his eyebrows, 'for the coolness of the breeze, and the summer grazings. Flies fair drove them crazy on the low land. If you didn't fetch them up by July, there was a plague on the beasts, bellowing and thrashing with the warble-fly, they were.' He laid an index-finger across his thumbnail. 'They'd creep up the nostrils of a cow, look, and spread the eggs out in the nose. Right up by the brain, they hatched. And the creature coughing maggots for days, until you cleaned her out. The midges, too, great grey clouds of them coming down on your head. I tell you, the shielings were the place to be.'

James's mind seethed with the idea of maggots thrusting up against the brain, and he shuddered.

'Sheep, man, that's what we're running nowadays; wool for the tweeds. Beastly stupid things that they are, but it's paying.' He spat sideways on to the dry turf, his spittle a white star of foam. 'Rachel Mackenzie has a cow, though, if you've a mind to see one. She's what you would be calling a farmer, I suppose! And I'm thinking we ought to be away down the hill, or there'll be some wonder at our where-abouts.'

'Are you going to see your aunt now?' He hadn't prepared himself for the idea of meeting anybody else, and he felt shy at the prospect.

'She'll no be looking to bite the head off you, so don't go worrying yourself.' The man lit a crumpled cigarette. 'One more breath of the fresh air, and it's away with us.'

They staggered down the uneven hillside clutching their hard burdens of peat, and repeated the journey until the back of the little car was laden.

The Beast jogged away along the coastal road, Alec sounding the horn as sheep wandered across his path. They came to a little summit, and he tapped the boy's arm. 'It's that fine a day, you can see Scotland.' He raised an elbow at the mainland in the distance.

Beside a low white house the car pulled up, the engine ticked to a halt.

'She doesna' receive many visitors,' said Alec, as if an apology was needed. There was a straggling area of vegetables planted in front of the house, fenced round with wires, and a gate made of planks nailed roughly together. A row of brown flaky sea-fish, split and mottled, were drying along the top of the fence.

'*Saithe*,' said the man. James swung the gate to, and picked his way through the potato plants and heat-shattered kale. The front door faced the road rather than the sea; it was set into the middle of the roughly plastered wall, with one small window to either side of it. The roof was thatched with twisted ropes of heather stalks, pulled down thick and tight and stitched across with cord. A line of large stones was suspended along the lower edge of the roof, to keep the tension. The effect was neat, and James had seen nothing like it; the single-storey buildings that his father developed on the estates down south appeared smaller and flimsier than this, but their slim roofs looked finished and less temporary.

'Built it myself,' said Alec, tapping his chest, 'once the grants came through. Before that, she lived in the black house.' He indicated a low building with dry-stone walls, to the left of the house, and entered his aunt's home without knocking.

There was smoke creeping from one of the twin chimneys. The boy was reluctant to walk in through the open door without invitation, so he stood there and looked in. The room was surprisingly large, and almost filled with furniture. An old woman sat next to the fire, on the far side of a broad kitchen table. She was looking at him in silence, through round, wire-rimmed spectacles.

Her nephew was standing beside her, and there were no introductions. Miss Mackenzie spoke to James as if resuming a conversation that had been naturally interrupted. '*Thig a nuas*: come up, now, Seumas, and sit you down. Don't be a stranger here, in this house.' Her head and shoulders were

32

wrapped in a pale shawl, and she wore a long black skirt, with an apron. From her appearance, he had expected her voice to be cracked and dry, but it was smooth and deep. The boy entered the room of the house with a tight smile. It smelled of smoke, with a sapid suggestion of oils. A dark-stained wooden dresser ran the length of the back wall, with books, bottles, glass floats and tins arranged in groups along its shelves. A small array of china plates was propped against the runners, with mugs and cups hanging below them.

'It was rescued from the sea,' said Miss Mackenzie, following the line of his eyes. 'That was taken from the SS *Atlanta*.' She sat in her chair by the flames, shaking slightly with age.

'Aye, dragged it up from the deeps, so she did, all on her own, the very day she finished the building of this house,' said Alec. His aunt ignored him stonily.

'It's a kindness, you should have helped this hopeless man here with the peats. With you up for your holidays, too. But now that you're here, you'll have the wee *strupag* in my house – just a cup of tea to be getting inside you.' Her movements were remarkably quick, as she rose from the chair and moved to the sideboard where plates were stacked, waiting.

Alec stretched by the fire, his braces unbuttoned, hands cupped behind his head.

'Would you like me to help?' ventured the boy. It was well past eleven, and he looked apprehensively at the considerable meal that Miss Mackenzie was arranging on the table before them. She had prepared drop-scones, and stacks of bread, and a cupful of pale paste.

'You could maybe fetch my pot there for the tea. It stands over by the side of the fire.' It was clear that her nephew was not intending to shift from his position of comfort. The boy carefully picked up a brown teapot and carried it to her in both hands. She tipped powdery tea into it and poured water from the kettle that was hooked over the fire. 'That's it, now,' she said.

They sat down. 'Have you many residing at the lodge?' she asked. 'It's a long time now since I was up there.'

'There's seven of us in all.'

'And that idle young Kirsty, is she feeding you up? You look that pale, I'm thinking she's no looking after you.' James felt embarrassed. He had heard his father complaining about the food, but he himself was a poor eater, and it had seemed delicious enough compared to what he was used to at school. He told Miss Mackenzie that he was having a marvellous time.

'You must eat. A fine fellow like yourself, with the growing upon you.' She placed the pot on the tablecloth, and a squirt of steam came from its spout. 'How old are you, Seumas?'

He told her he was almost twelve.

'Gu dearbh, yes indeed,' she said in confirmation. James sat upright, hands in his lap, his back not touching the chair over which was hung a length of foxy-coloured tweed. She tilted a plateful of woolly white bread at him, and steered over a jar of jam with a plain label which said 'Co-op' in blue letters.

'I'm not pretending I made either of these, mind. That bread there comes all the way from Glasgow – there's none of the island in it – and they say the jam is made from strawberries. Alec purchases it for me at the mobile shop. It tastes of medicine.' James spread some dutifully on his bread, and waited.

'Pieces of wood, they do say,' explained Alec, swinging himself upright and towards the table. 'That's what jam is made from. Reminds me of the army.' He began to plaster a scone with the glutinous pink confection.

'That cigarette's smoke will be bound to improve it, I suppose?'

He pinched out the glowing tip with an exaggerated scowl. 'You'll be getting like Christina, Auntie, and God forbid there shall be two of you. I've told you times enough; I'll give up the habit just as soon as I can.' He pushed some bright food into his mouth, eyebrows raised at his aunt.

'I heard the wind, but I did not see it.' She shrugged her cheeks, the proud bones of her face looking stern under the white wings of her hair. James chewed over his mouthful of bread with difficulty, filling one cheek with hot tea and letting it seep through the mixture to help him swallow it. He could not work out if the old woman was really angry.

'It gives me my energy, the smoking.' Alec gleamed in conspiracy at the boy, which made him look down quickly.

'There's no smoke in the lark's house,' pronounced Miss Mackenzie, presiding over the table, eating nothing.

Alec coughed in to his cup. 'Sayings! Always the same. An old saying for every occasion.' He pointed at her with a biscuit. 'Now that's enough, I'm telling you. Or I'll perhaps be away home with your peats in the back of my car, and forget to stack them up for you.' He wiggled the biscuit defiantly in the air, but his aunt ignored him. She stacked three drop-scones on James's plate and scooped a spoonful of crowdie on the top. The boy looked at his recently-cleared plate in dismay.

'Go on with you,' she said encouragingly. 'Don't you want the colour in your cheeks?' He nibbled slowly at the sour, soft cheese.

'It's all the way up from Guildford you've come?' The question took James by surprise. Miss Mackenzie pronounced the place-name as two distinct words. She was smiling keenly at him.

'Er, yes. It's quite near London.'

'It won't have moved many miles since I was there, then.' He looked at her in astonishment, forgetting his manners. Crowdie drooped from his scone, and sank down on to the plate.

She nodded at him to continue eating. 'Balcombe Park, that's where I was. Do you know the place at all?' She had the same small blue eyes of her nephew.

The boy shook his head, unable to think clearly. The room seemed suddenly close, and the situation impossible. He wished Alec would interrupt.

35

'It's near to Guildford itself, at least it was when I was a girl. Eighteen-ninety-six was the year I moved down there, to work in the household of Sir Frederick Maitland. Every summer he would come up here around these islands, cruising in his steam-powered yacht: great parties of gentlemen there were, from the south, and their fine ladies with him, as often as not looking out for a maid or some new member of staff. It was better than the sight of a basket full of herrings to clean every morning, I'm telling you. Three years I was down there, and me twenty-six years of age when I left this island for the first time.'

Looking at the tangled back of her hands, and the drawn flesh of her cheeks, James found it impossible to imagine her as a woman that young. He had never heard of Balcombe Park, and he felt sure she must be entirely confused. He found himself staring at her; he wondered exactly how old she might be.

'Did you want to come back?' he asked.

'It was that long ago,' interrupted Alec quietly, 'and a world of changes gone between.'

'I wished to return when the time came, yes, and it's here that I have been ever since.' She busied herself with the teapot.

'If you're wanting me to stack yon peats for you, Auntie, I'd best be away to fetch them, or Christina will be ready with my meal, and me not home yet.'

'She'll be thinking you've the drink taken.'

'What, in this house? That would be a day indeed.' He pushed back his chair, and the boy stood up with him. Miss Mackenzie looked indignant.

'You're surely not taking the boy out for more work?'

'He's a mind of his own; practically the grown man.' They both looked at James, standing politely to attention, puzzled by the unfamiliar tones of the conversation. He was not sure if either of them was joking, but then Alec pushed his way out of the room, leaving the door swinging in the sun. The boy watched him go, and turned to the woman. A softness came into her face.

'Never be minding him, Seumas. Always a one for the grumbles. You've your tea to finish, yet.' Once more he sat down.

'There's three weeks more of your stay here, then?' Miss Mackenzie seemed to know a lot about the arrangements at Graeval. He told her of the other guests who were staying, and what parts of the country they came from; how they were all interested in the fishing, or the shooting of grouse, but he'd never done it himself, and his father still thought he was too young. She listened to his news intently. James found it easy to talk to her of such things, as he held his teacup and looked at her room.

'I'm meant to be working quite a lot of the time, actually,' he continued. 'Mr Luxmoore – my form-teacher – he told Daddy I needed to do extra reading.' He did not tell her this was because he was due to sit the scholarship exam for Harrow.

'Don't you go ignoring those books, mind, just because you've an island to explore and a foolish man to guide you, who lives by the dreams of his head.' She flapped a hand in mock admonition.

'Well,' he began doubtfully, 'Alec said to spend the time discovering things about the island, while I had the chance, because I'd learn more that way. About things that really matter.' He was not sure if he was being disloyal, but he could sense the woman's affection beneath the criticism of her nephew.

She slipped the shawl off her head in irritation, revealing a fine hair-net. 'And much good it ever did him. *Gloir mhor an colainn bhig* – great talk in a small body. There's truth can be had from books, and a pleasure in it, too, if you've the mind. But on the hill,' she paused, 'sometimes, there is only the wind.'

James fidgeted in his chair. He was hoping Alec would soon be finished, so they could get back to the lodge.

'Alec showed me his lobster boat. They caught twelve. We

37

had one for supper.' He was uncertain if she wanted him to get up and leave. 'It was a big one,' he added.

'There's no the harvest in the sea that there was,' she replied drily. 'That's the way of things. Out here in my father's lifetime, on *Am Bide Buidhe* – the yellow point by the house, look, that was the place you could pick the scallops off the shore so big you'd to cut the flesh into four different pieces before you could eat it. *Madadh uisge*, he called them: "water dogs", to look at the size of them. But the baskets they fetch home now. Poor things with hardly a bite in each, and them going half the way to Norway to pull them up. *Moran shligean's beagan bhiadhan* – many shells and little meat.'

Miss Mackenzie stood up and began to gather plates towards her. He saw she was wearing a pair of men's work-boots without any laces. James began to help her to clear the table.

'When I returned from the south of England,' she said, one hand poised, 'the waters around this island were the finest for the fishing in the whole of Europe. You couldn't see the houses of Stornoway for the oak-smoke coming across the harbour from the curers; and us for a mile around the pier, gutting and sorting the silvery fish into barrels.' She picked the uneaten food off the plates and stored it away in two biscuit-tins, shooing the boy lightly to one side.

'And then we'd follow the shoals, we herring-girls. Up to the Shetlands, and round the way to Great Yarmouth until the season was out, and our hands as red as the legs of an oyster-catcher from all the cutting and scraping. But you'd not find ten crews in the island today.'

'I stood on the shore of Loch Erisort one year with my sister Peigi, that was Alec's mother, and you could scoop them out in a bucket, and never need to wet your feet for moving. The noise of them out there in the sea was like a rustling, they were that thick swimming together in their millions. A whole field of herrings, leaving a thin froth like a frost on the surface from their belling.'

The idea of water being that full of fish rather disturbed

James. It reminded him of something out of the Bible, or a crammed painting of prehistoric times, with gigantic striped squid and long crabs the size of logs. He had seen such pictures in books and periodicals at school, but he felt sure the woman's memory was exaggerating.

She leaned on the table, peering at the low fire. 'My father was the greatest finder of the fish at night: he could tell in the dark what type was a single fish leaping, from the sound of it. And he'd take me out with him on the wherry, and we'd lie there on our stomachs and listen. When the sea had the fire of a summer's night glowing in it, he would rattle the anchor and watch for the blue flash of the king herring turning down deep at the noise. And in a winter's daytime they burned red in the water. Like blood.'

Alec stood in the doorway. 'Living off the foam of their own tails, too, I'll be bound.' He laughed at her. 'Never a thing to be found in their stomachs when you had them for gutting, Auntie, is that not right now?'

She regarded him slowly. 'You were grateful enough for what your grandfather brought back for us, wrapped in his oilskins, that much I do mind, Alec Campbell. Before you learned all your wisdom. Heaven help us if we'd to live off the catches you'd bring home.'

'There's food to be had from the shops now, Auntie, and glad I am of it, too. Herrings! Horrible oily things.' He dabbed his jaw with a sleeve, and winked. 'Come along, now, big fellow. We must be away to the lodge.'

Miss Mackenzie roused herself and started for the door, making noises like a bird.

'They'll be blaming me, so they will. Your mummy and daddy; wondering wherever have you been.'

The boy stood in the chill moment. He saw the thin cheek of a woman bending, the hair moving dark red above him. 'My mother is not here,' he said. 'She's not well. She lives in a different place, down south.' It was the fomula he had been given, and there was no sense in wishing. 'She's ill.'

Miss Mackenzie plaited a shape in the air, but said nothing. He said goodbye to her, and his face began to feel hot.

'Promise you'll come again to visit the *cailleach*, the old woman?' The raised knuckles of her hand bobbed at him as she followed them out into the sunlight, her shawl trailing down her back like a hood. James said yes, he would come back. They closed the gate, and the little line of fish lurched on the wire.

It might have been the sticky food, or maybe something else, but after a few minutes in the car he felt sick. He tucked his head out of the window, and the hot breeze ballooned in his ears and swept down his collar. Alec was telling some story and waving his hands above the wheel as they went, but he could hear nothing from the inside of the car. His ears were roaring as if to the sound of flames.

VI

'My son tells me you were in the desert, Campbell. Which regiment?' Richard Benson was assembling the three sections of his shotgun, inspecting the interior gleam of the barrels. He did not look at the man standing in the doorway with the whining dogs. It was the Twelfth of August; even breakfast had finished a half-hour early.

'Fifth Battalion, 51st Division Seaforth Highlanders,' said Alec, with an automatic briskness. 'Sir.' The long-haired setters were standing up against the strain of the twisted leashes. They could smell the oil off the guns.

'I see. And, what happened? Eh?' He flicked the walnut stock in the direction of the man's legs. Alec hauled on both arms, and the dogs were swung backwards to his side, white-ridged tongues flapping. 'Thrown into a crater, sir, during the shelling. In forty-two. I was riding a dispatch cycle. My leg was broken.' There was challenge, rather than self-pity, in the quietness of his reply.

'An accident. I see. Bad luck.' Benson tested the ejector-mechanism of his weapon, and buffed the metal with the suede patch on his jacket. 'I was with the First Surreys, myself. In many ways a most interesting war; but we didn't reach Africa until later. Operation Torch. Just after you were, you know. Injured. Fill this belt for me, would you?' He slid a bandolier and a carton of cartridges along the pitted surface of the table.

Alec sounded almost apologetic. 'I'm just a wee bit tied up with these boys at present.'

Benson finally gave him the benefit of a glance. 'Ah, quite. I'm sure I can manage.' He began stuffing the ammunition into the loops of the belt. 'We had a special battle patrol –

you might have known some of them, keepers and ghillies, that sort of thing. Formed in 'forty; first-rate pioneers. Chap called Woodhouse in command.' He rummaged around in the box. 'Fair number of poachers in that troop, too. Deadly they were as snipers.'

'My wife's cousin, now, he was with them. Calum Macleod was his name. He died at Cassino.'

'Yes. A terrible business. Dreadful conditions; rain, and so on. Brave lot.'

'Bracken,' hissed Alec, giving the leather a jerk. 'Hup, there.' The dog wound its lead around his leg, and he staggered sideways with a little hop. The setter looked unrepentant, and Alec pressed down its back with his knees. 'Patience, man.'

'All set?' Geoffrey Willis proceeded into the gun-room clutching his boots. 'Won't be half a tick. Morning, Campbell. What d'ye think – enough breeze for the scent?' Humming, he began to lace his feet into the leather.

'Difficult to say, Doctor, before we make the higher ground. But we might happen upon a bird or two, after a walk for them.'

'Well, I for one am dispensing with my tie right here and now. Too hot out there; bad for the circulation.' He rubbed his hands at them both.

Benson slid his gun into its canvas sling. 'Grant tells me the birds on Mircavat are still rather small. Loads of "cheepers", is that right?'

'I couldn't rightly say. It's weeks since I was up there.' Alec shook his head.

'Quite so,' said Benson. 'Now. Let's see how the others are shaping up.'

'Oh, I wouldn't be in too much of a rush, Richard,' Dr Willis grunted, tugging at his laces. 'Old Bobby's in a lather. Wouldn't you know? Blaming it all on Alice. Can't find his sacred puttees, and swears he can't hit a barn door without them. Or a barn, either, shouldn't wonder.'

James stood out by the blue Land Rover, gouging moss from between the cobblestones. He was wearing his new pair of corduroys, tucked into Wellington boots.

'Reckon it'll rain?' asked Cooper, cuffing him on the shoulder, laughing at his own remark. The sky above the courtyard looked hard and clear. The man swung a heavy cartridge-bag into the back of the car. 'Tell you what, young man. We'll have a little bet: if it rains on any of us today, I'll give you a ten-bob note.' The boy's eyes widened. 'Done?' They shook hands. 'But – Mum's the word. You know what your father thinks about betting.' He held a finger to his lip.

Bobby Paton came lumbering across the yard. 'Got them. Ready for the off.' He disappeared into the gun-room for his equipment.

'All aboard,' beckoned the head keeper, standing by the car in his immaculate checked tweeds. James huddled into the back of the vehicle, the dogs clambering nervously over him, panting like engines. He had a canvas game-bag slung across one shoulder, with netting stitched to the outside. The white, waterproofed lining was smeared with the brown of last season's blood.

'Glorious Twelfth', said Paton, his puttees in place. He adjusted the tilt of his cap and nodded to the boy. 'Let's get to work.'

Though he had never seen a grouse, James had accompanied his father several times to pheasant-shoots in Surrey, and he enjoyed the trips. On those days, spent entirely in his father's company, he felt he was being of use to him, carrying the heavy, beautiful birds after each drive. His father was a good shot, and had promised to buy him a gun of his own, if he passed his scholarship; but the idea of shooting things himself held little appeal. He preferred to observe – the elaborate organisation of the beaters, and the team of dog-handlers waiting to retrieve, and the driving from stand to stand was exciting to him, like being part of an army. For the most part, he could be silent, and watch the pheasants tumble like fireworks above the trees.

The four guns formed a line, with Grant in the middle attached to Bracken. Now that they were actually on the hill, the dog seemed less impatient, his head nodding up into the faint breeze. They moved slowly away from the road, with James and Alec following some yards behind, managing lunch-bags, game-bags, and the second setter. 'You'll be wanting this,' he said, handing the boy a crooked stick. 'And take your time, man. I'm no carrying you, along with the rest of it.'

There were few boulders on this part of the moor, but the dry heather was thick and wiry, and it needed a high step to avoid tripping. Their boots sent up billows of fine pollen. When they reached the first knoll, Grant stopped and unleashed his dog, which stood attentively while the keeper laid a hand under its throat. He had a tall stick with a stag's-horn head, into the tip of which was carved a whistle. As a reminder, he blew it, once, by Bracken's ear, and waved the dog away across the heather with a sweep of his arm.

For a quarter of an hour they worked steadily along the hill, but the only birds that rose were larks, streaming steeply away into the air before them. Then, ranging some distance to the left in front, Bracken swerved quickly in the middle of his run and began to creep forwards, his tail beating gradually slower.

'He's feeling into the scent, now,' said Grant, not taking his eyes off the dog, which had halted by a wide clump of bog-myrtle, his tail stiffened, and his left paw raised from the ground. The men approached, two guns on either side of the quivering setter. 'That's you, boy,' whispered the keeper, pulling gently at Bracken's ear. Scanning the ground in anticipation of the explosion of wings, the formation moved slowly in the direction the dog's nose indicated.

Suddenly, Grant brought his stick down with a crack, and a high squeal blared from the foliage. 'Wasting our time, you bugger,' he told the dog. He bent down, and by its hind legs pulled from the myrtle the coiled body of a rabbit, its

44

backbone arched, ears flattened, screaming. He twisted the neck into silence. 'Apologies, gentlemen,' he said, 'that myrtle proper kills the scent.'

'False alarm, everyone.' Dr Willis rubbed his neck with a handkerchief. 'Not to worry, eh?'

Bobby Paton looked bored. 'Not exactly a flying start to the season.' Nobody answered him.

At the next point, a covey of five dark birds rose skirring away, and three promptly fell with a spurt of feathers. The shots made a muffled sound as they passed into the heather with little echo, despite the stillness of the air. 'Share and share alike,' Alec said, handing the boy one of the grouse. The brown plumage tapered into white down, over its legs and claws, like spats. James held the walnut of the bird's head and examined the red rings around its eyes, the tough beak. He shook it down into the folds of the bag.

.   .   .   .   .

Carrying the sharp knife, with its deep triangular blade, she opened the wooden gate and walked through the uneven growths of the vegetable patch. She stooped easily and began to saw at the crispy stem of the kale, straightening slowly once its banner of leaves came away freely in her hand.

There was a black plastic bucket outside the door, from which she retrieved five small potatoes, their reddish skins powdered with chocolatey earth. These vegetables she placed on the wooden board next to the chicken, its broken tubular neck scrawled like something that had buckled in the heat. It had been plucked earlier that morning, and now she carefully opened its vent and began to worm her forefinger around inside it, looking not at the chicken but at the sea beyond the window, her finger feeling its way until she had hold of the glutinous entrails. She drew these out on to the board with a slow sucking sound.

Separating out the giblets that she needed for cooking, she cut the trunk of the bird into several pieces and crossed to the fireplace where already a pot was set over the flame. There was dulse floating on the surface of the bubbling water, exuding a thin greenish foam, and she squeezed the sodden mass against the side of the pot with the back of the spoon, pressing out the juices.

'*Deiseil, Deiseil,*' she said aloud as she stirred the mixture with strong clockwise motions.

Above her on the mantelpiece the brass ship's clock gave out a steady dripping sound, and through the open door she could also hear, from the hill, way beyond, a volley of shots faintly disturbing the morning.

.   .   .   .   .

By the time they broke for lunch, he was happily exhausted, with ten grouse in his bag. They settled on the shore of a little lochan, and Grant counted the crumpled birds. 'Eleven brace in all,' he reported, looking pleased.

'A very good morning; well done,' said Cooper. He produced a large hip-flask, bound in crocodile, with a round stopper. The silver casing slid off the bottom, to make a cup, and he splashed whisky into it.

'Aye, well, thank you very much indeed, sir. There was some grand shooting, though, that I saw.' Grant laughed obsequiously, and raised the drink towards the assembled company. '*Slainte,*' he proclaimed.

'I say, I hope there's some of that left for us, old man,' said Dr Willis, looking genuinely worried. He was slumped against a rock, shirt-sleeves rolled up, fanning himself with a deer-stalker. 'I haven't come trekking up here for nothing, you know.'

Benson lobbed a cartridge into the man's chest. 'If you were a slightly better advertisement for your profession, Geoffrey, you'd be quicker off the mark all round. Then maybe you'd get the gun up to your shoulder before all the birds have been shot.'

'Well, really.'

Alec and the boy handed out the lunch-boxes, as the flask was passed round. The head keeper stood, hands on his hips, like a referee, approving the banter. He was relieved that the men were in a good mood, for they had seen fewer birds than he had really expected.

'So. Geoffrey. Want to consult the Admiral?' Cooper smiled at the reclining man.

'What's that you say?'

Waving his flask, he repeated, 'The Admiral. Would you like a word?'

'Ah, well. Not more than a stag's breath, mind.' He accepted the cup, without moving, and smacked it to his lips. 'Odd name for a flask, though.'

'Tell him, Michael. Better get it over with.' Benson sounded weary.

They began to unwrap their sandwiches, while the two keepers, the ritual of the dram completed, retired to eat their own lunch at a polite distance.

'Well, you see, Geoffrey; unlike you, some of us had to leave the country during the war.' Dr Willis had remained a civilian in Wiltshire throughout, and it was there that James's father had met him, while on leave. The others laughed at this embellishment to a joke they had all heard before.

'Am I going to enjoy this story, I wonder?' enquired the doctor.

'On one occasion, I found myself on the bridge of a destroyer in a rough old storm, and, being a cavalry man myself, I naturally felt a bit worried. As you can imagine. So I asked the captain of the tub if he was planning to alter course, and he said he'd have to go down and consult the Admiral before making a decision. Well, I'd no idea we were carrying top brass. Turned out we weren't. The bridge reeked of grog when he returned, and the third time he tried it I said I'd come with him. The chap was just using it as an excuse to sneak in a snifter, to steady his nerves.'

James laughed happily at the dumbshow of astonishment

which the doctor performed for his benefit. His father capped the story, 'Which is why you steered Jeremy into the RAF and away from the senior service, I take it?' The Coopers' son, who would otherwise have been in the party, had just begun his National Service.

'Precisely.' They began to eat.

Lochan Dubh, the 'black loch', was studded with water-lilies in full flower. The patches of water in between were so dark that they barely reflected the sun. Diminutive trout made dimples from time to time in the centre, but otherwise the surface was still. Long-legged flies skated and stopped around the crisp floating leaves.

Pinching crumbs meticulously off his herringbone breeches, Bobby Paton frowned at his knees. 'Hope the girls have found that place Grant told them about. I really must have a new suit. This lot won't see me through another season.'

'Gone shopping, have they?' asked Willis. 'Can't for the life of me think where.'

'Nothing as grand as a shop, no, no. Mrs Macleod's was all they said. Makes it herself, in a shed. Apparently, she's the best on the island, sends tweed all over the world, as fast as she can weave it. I just hope Alice isn't in one of her charitable moods. I told her to bargain. The stuff's bound to be cheaper up here; simple economics.'

'I suppose Grant forgot to mention that Campbell's wife has a loom,' said James's father. It was not a question.

'Well, that's odd; it would be much closer, apart from anything else.'

'No love lost between those two men, unless I'm mistaken. Midges have found us.' He slapped his cheek. 'Oh yes. Grant gave me the run-down on Sunday. Said Campbell was a typical islander – lazy as hell and a devil for the hard stuff. He's from the mainland, himself.'

The boy sat listening, storing those adult secrets which had the cadence of truth in the assured way they were being shared. He remembered the old woman's remark about the drink, but it seemed that everyone was drinking a lot now they were on the island.

'Campbell expected to succeed his father as head-keeper, apparently, but of course his mishap during the war put paid to that,' continued Benson. 'Kershaw kept him on out of loyalty, let him keep the car, and so on. But ever since Grant was imported from Caithness Campbell always resented him. Does the bare minimum.' He drew a cigar from its metal tube, and twirled it next to his ear.

'It sounds exceedingly probable,' agreed Paton. 'You only have to look at the state of the place. Shocking. The whole island is a shambles, come to that. Did you notice those houses, as we drove here? Refuse heaped by the road, gardens chock full of weeds. It's not as if there's much else to occupy them, after all.'

'It's a poor soil, Bobby. Just consider it.'

'Maybe. But it used to support thousands of people. They've just neglected it. Strikes me as criminal.'

Dr Willis stirred heavily. 'Can't imagine it was ever a very comfy spot, by the looks of it.' His eyes were closed.

'Good God, Geoffrey. I do believe you're a Liberal.'

'Not me, Richard; you've got the wrong man.' He moved his hands in a disclaimer, and resumed his nap.

'There are grants, after all.' Paton had worked himself into a state of indignation. 'Look at the rest of Scotland. I refuse to believe there aren't fertilizers and things, even for peat. This isn't the desert – Good God, you could grow plenty of crops here, given a little willpower and imagination.'

'What's all this, a conspiracy?' interrupted Cooper, coming over from his seat by the recumbent Willis. 'Afraid I've bored the good doctor to sleep. I'll give him ten minutes, and then wake him up with my twelve-bore. Top-up, anyone?'

His partner shook his head. 'Not for me. Bobby here's been reading me chapter and verse on how to develop this island's economy. He's got all the answers, you know.'

'I've been giving it a little thought, myself. As we were

49

coming up the hill. I reckon you could pick up this whole estate for peanuts, as the Yanks say. Extend the lodge – no use sleeping eight, not big enough. Slap down a few pre-fabs, maybe. Make it a retreat – "exclusive sporting haven in the unspoilt Hebrides." That sort of thing.' Cooper raised an arm expansively.

Benson looked dismissive. 'Not a chance. People want to go abroad, see the world. The Comet. Exotic resorts. Besides, it would take you a lifetime to get the work done up here.'

'Why hasn't Kershaw done it already, if it's such a good idea?' Paton looked beadily at them.

'He couldn't be less interested,' replied Cooper. 'He's only been up here once since the old man died. Lives in France somewhere, and there's nothing in it for him. He doesn't need the money. Look at that glassworks of theirs.'

'You could be right,' said Benson doubtfully, 'but it would need proper planning. Scout round the island, and see what's what. It's a thought.'

They were interrupted by the keepers coming over to fetch them. The setters barked, a rough yellow noise inflaming the afternoon.

·   ·   ·   ·   ·

'Good show,' Rosemary Cooper had exclaimed when his father announced it over tea the following day. They had been out in the launch, and were hungry. 'It will be lovely to see Venetia again. What a surprise.'

There was no hollowness in the way she said it, and the others hummed their approval.

'She will be arriving on the mid-day ferry; James and I can drive up to meet her,' said Benson. 'It will be an opportunity to see the north of the island.'

'I'm sure she'll adore it,' Rosemary said, 'and such a good place, I imagine, for the light.'

Dr Willis was tearing enthusiastically at his bannock.

'Splendid! Another pretty girl to swell the ranks. Well done, Richard.' Crumbs spilled from his mouth as he smiled.

James was scraping the chocolate coating off his biscuit, using his bottom teeth like a plane. He knew that his own approval was not required, and the news was not really surprising. Venetia Walker was a frequent visitor to their house even though his mother, once her close friend, was no longer living at home. The Walkers had a weekend cottage nearby, and she had taken upon herself the supervision of the Bensons' garden, since James's father had no interest in flowers. In spring and summer, Mrs Walker was regularly to be seen strolling with her secateurs and basket through their walled garden, or crouching in the white border labelling the new plants she had ordered.

He was not especially pleased to hear she was coming to stay. She paid a lot of attention to James when he was in their company, but he found her overpowering, with her flamboyant clothes and her husky voice. And he was still frightened of her son, Guy.

The unrelieved closeness of the weather had changed slightly over night. A shrewd wind was coming off the sea and along the shore it was cooler, although still no clouds interrupted the sun. After tea, he went out looking for shells with Alice Paton. She had asked him to show her the beach he had discovered, because she thought she might decorate some cigar-boxes by sticking on as many different shells as they could find. They would make, she explained, such nice souvenirs.

Carrying a bucket they had borrowed from the kitchen, the boy led her around the bay and on to the back of the peninsula. Alice walked very slowly, picking her way fastidiously along the rocks.

'We'll have to stop for a little breather,' she said. 'I'm quite out of breath already.' She sat tidily down on the headland. The tide was lunging in, the long waves coming along the hardness of the coast.

'What a smell!' she declared, tilting back her little head. 'Isn't it glorious?'

Two herring-gulls stalked around the promontory, their heads flicking from side to side like groundsmen scouring for litter. The rock was splashed with the white crab-shapes of their droppings.

'It's come too far in already,' said James. 'We won't even find limpets up here. We ought to go straight to the beach.'

Alice looked at him vaguely. 'I know. Yes. I know. One second more.' She seemed to have forgotten the purpose of the expedition. There was a small handkerchief tucked into the cuff of her blouse, and she teased it out slowly, like a conjuror. 'You know, it's a long time since I met anyone in such a hurry as you. Old ladies like myself need to take their time. I'm sorry.' She turned the handkerchief over and over in her hands.

He had no way of telling exactly, but James certainly couldn't think of her as old. She might perhaps have been forty, he did not know; but she did look tired. It was as though coming outside into the air had dried her up, whisking the already faint colour from her cheeks. 'Let's go,' said Alice Paton. 'Let's go, and collect those shells.'

'Look, there,' shouted James. He ran along the rock, waving at the place, the hole that was closing in the water.

'What is it? What on earth did you see?'

'It was huge. It wasn't a fish. There was only the tail.'

'Oh dear. Perhaps it was a whale, or something really dangerous.' Alice went and took his hand, and started to pull him away from the sea. 'Whatever it was, it's gone now.'

James looked radiant with excitement. 'A seal. I'm sure it must have been a great big seal. Alec will know – I'll ask him.' He swung the bucket vigorously as he scanned the waves, but nothing else broke the surface.

They clambered gently over the hump of the peninsula, and there lay the curved beach like the wing of a bird, foam sliding on to it in a creamy hiss. Almost half the sand was already under water. 'We'll have to be incredibly quick,' he said, 'or we'll never find any. You take the bucket, and I'll try at the other end.' He ran off along the beach.

Within ten minutes, both the pockets of his grey flannel shorts were stuffed with shells; he picked them up indiscriminately as he went along the high-water line. They were mostly small, and clean, but from time to time he collected an especial prize – the flattened, butterfly shape of a certain bivalve that inside showed a faint salmon-glow, a delicate sheen of pink. These he put carefully apart, in the pocket of his shirt.

When he turned back to retrace his steps, Alice Paton had disappeared. James ran back along the sand, and climbed on to the rocks, but he could not see her anywhere. He could see all the way round to the lodge, but there was no one. Clawing his way up the dunes behind, he stood uneasily on top and looked up and down the grassy meadow that stretched behind, the marram grass humming in the breeze; but she was not there, either.

You can't fall into the sea, thought James, from a sandy beach. There was no sign, either, of the bucket. He sat and paddled his way down the back of the dune, and lay there, listening to the breeze skating over the pale sand, thin grass curling off it like the hair from a wrist. He was glad once more to be alone.

The marram land in front of him was bobbing with yellow flowers. Alec had told him that you could taste the flowers in the milk from cows that grazed the *machair* but there were no beasts there that he could see. He pressed his ear against the dune and listened to the submarine rumbling of his blood. Out here, where he had slid down out of their sight, they would not find him – not Alice Paton, nor his father, nor Venetia Walker, when she came. It was to be his secret.

There was a place like it that he had in the school grounds, at the far end of the Chapel Wood, where the rhododendrons gave way into a little dip, full of pine-needles and leaves. The afternoon that Walker had ruined his boat, he had gone there to be alone; after ten minutes of crouching, pulling his fingers and shrugging himself out of his anger, he had emerged with the fear of it left behind him. Guy Walker was a bully, a year older than James. Because he was in the class above, he usually ignored the younger boy, but sometimes in the passage he would just push him as they passed, sending him on to the shoe-racks, because he was clever, and Walker was not. Once, in the changing-rooms, Walker had slugged him across the neck with a linen-bag full of wet clothes.

Uncle Henry had sent him a wooden yacht that summer, one that he had carved himself. It had rigging, and a metal keel, and a little pennant with the boy's initials inked on it. After swimming was finished on the weekends, they could sail their boats in the pool before tea, and the first Sunday that James had launched his new toy, it had drawn the envy of the others who were there.

When he opened his locker the next morning to fetch his pencil-case before lessons, the boat had been attacked. The three masts were snapped off, and there was glue poured all over the hull, which had made the paint run. All the edges of the model had been hacked off with a craft-knife: the shavings still littered the locker.

James had not told the master on duty; he realised there was nothing to be done. He did not want Uncle Henry to discover what had happened to his present. When the room was empty, he took the disfigured wreck, and placed it, along with the shorn wood, in the middle of a newspaper, which he wrapped up into a parcel. He buried the lot in his secret place in Chapel Wood, and there it remained.

The boy stood up and shook the sand from his clothes. He walked along the foot of the dunes, away from the direction of the lodge. In the distance, he could see a dribble of smoke from the chimney of a small house standing on the edge of the *machair*. For a moment, he imagined it might be where Alec lived, and he quickened his pace. He wanted to consult the man about the creature that was plunging in the bay.

In front of the building stood a child who looked a few years younger than James himself. He was wearing a brown smock, and tight trousers that reached to his calves, but he had no shoes on. His complexion was shiny and dark, as if already rubbed by the wind, and his hair reached almost to his shoulders. A smell of something cooking drifted over from the house. No sound came from inside, and the place did not seem to have any windows.

James stared at the child for a moment, wishing they had not made such abrupt contact, and they did not speak to each other. The child stood and watched James as he turned away, scaled the dunes, and slithered back down to the beach.

Feet from where he landed, was Alice Paton. She was holding the bucket, with a few low inches of shells inside, and she looked at him furiously.

'I was looking for you,' he explained, 'but you disappeared. Look what I've found.' He dug a hand into his breast-pocket, and cupped the pink shells towards her. 'Look.'

She knocked them out of his palm with the back of her hand. 'Don't you ever play a trick on me like that again,' she breathed at him. 'You unpleasant little boy.'

James was amazed at her reaction. 'But I couldn't find you,' he protested. 'I came looking.' He knelt down and began to retrieve the shells from the warm beach.

'I went out of my mind,' she said, 'with worry. Do you realise what time it is? You've been gone for hours.' She thrust a wrist at him, tapping the glass of her watch.

The boy looked her directly in the face. He thought they had been separated for fifteen minutes at the most, but what she said was true; it was now almost seven o'clock. He could not understand it, but he realised he must have fallen asleep. There was nothing for it; he would have to apologise and accept her anger, but he promised himself he would never take her with him again.

'Where have you *been*?' she repeated, clutching the lapels of her blouse with her left hand.

'I'm sorry,' he mumbled, staring at the little bucket. 'I fell asleep, I think. Sorry.'

'You're a liar,' said Alice Paton shrilly. She snatched the bucket from his grasp. 'Give those to me. They're mine. Just leave me alone.'

VII

'You have three alternatives,' his father had informed him the previous night. 'You may come with us, provided there is room. You may stay here and get on with some of that reading. Or you may accompany Campbell in the launch, and make yourself useful. The choice is yours. Either way you are not to go wandering off, scaring people to death. Do I make the position clear?'

The prospect of spending a hot day driving around the island, with lunch in the hotel, did not appeal greatly to James; but he was careful not to let this register in his expression. 'Well,' he had said, looking as doubtful as possible, 'I *would* like to try some fishing.'

'Then you must spend Sunday, at least, with your books.'

'All right, Father.'

Already he was growing tired of the daily expedition following the guns. He longed to be left to his own devices, but since the incident on the beach there had been a change in his father's attitude towards him; it was not something he precisely understood, for nothing definite had been said, but the boy was aware of some vague tension when the party was together at mealtimes. There had been no opportunity for simple explanations.

'I wouldn't take it to heart,' Dr Willis had said to him casually, but out of the blue. They were attempting to play croquet on the scrubby lawn. 'Little misunderstanding, happens to all of us. You know.' He ruffled the boy's hair reassuringly. 'I've actually had a word with Alice – with Mrs Paton – and it's best forgotten. She's just a wee bit nervous, that's all. Quite common. No children of her own, you see, and gets a touch agitated.' He bent over the cracked yellow

ball, and flicked his mallet several times before striking.
'There!'

The sightseeing party had already left when Alec arrived
the next morning. He seemed subdued, and the brightness
was out of his eyes, though he affected cheeriness.

'So, it's the two of us against the waves today, boy?' he
said. He made no effort to get out of his car. 'Have you your
piece?' James showed him the satchel containing his sandwiches and vacuum flask. 'Well, there's no sense us waiting.
There hasna' been a cod caught in this yard as long as I can
mind.'

The man said very little during their journey, and when he
did speak his mouth sounded pasty and dry.

'I've the boat brought round to my house. But we'll no be
away with the tackle before that wife of mine has you into
the kitchen, that's certain.' Alec flung his cigarette out of the
window, unfinished.

The board on his front gate read 'Number 4', though there
was not another house in sight. A large speckled sheep-dog,
one of its eyes turned white with age, hurled itself against the
length of cord that secured it to the porch as they approached.
Alec ignored the dog, and made for the corrugated shed
beyond.

'Come in and meet the spider,' he beckoned from the
doorway.

His wife was sitting on a long plank behind an elaborate
loom, which almost filled the place entirely. Dozens of thin
woollen threads were strung in a warp on the frame in front
of it.

'What's this, Christina? Resting from your web is it, and
you hardly begun?' Alec pointed a finger at the few inches of
completed cloth behind the shuttle. The woman slipped down
off her perch; she was wearing a house-coat, and had plump
black hair. James shook hands with her and said hello.

'Welcome to the centre of the tweed industry,' said
Christina.

'It looks awfully complicated.'

Alec lifted him up and set him down on the padded plank, his feet just touching the pedals. 'Away you go, then, and see for yourself.' He showed the boy how to activate the springs that sent the wooden shuttle flying across the warp. The machine worked with a pounding clatter; James was alarmed at the speed with which the intricate parts were operating in full view. It was like staring into the engine of a car while it was in motion.

He stopped pedalling after only a couple of minutes. 'There now,' said Alec, 'you're the weaver too.'

'Thank you. It was fun.' He did not want to hurt their feelings.

'Ach, no,' said Christina, 'it's maybe all right for an hour or so, but it's awful boring when you've got to be at it all day. I hate the noise. And these commercial patterns they want at the Association; well, take a look at them.' She patted one of the five rolls of cloth on the shelf. 'Herring-bone grey, and hound's-tooth, and checks that loud you can practically hear them.'

'Yes. It must be hard work.'

'Well, it wouldn't be bad if we had the power. But it has to be done by hand, or it can't be sold with the mark,' said Alec. 'Ridiculous regulations.' He rolled the contours of his words contemptuously. 'It's not as if it was a proper hand-loom anyway, the Hattersley. When my father had his old one, the *beart-mhor*, he'd the shuttle to throw by hand – twenty-seven inches across for every woof. For the breadth of the cloth. And then you had the web to shrink by hand, with them all singing the waulking songs, and pretending to enjoy it. I don't know.'

'Here, Seumas,' said Christina, 'this will do for the fishing.' She handed him a brightly-knitted woollen hat with a green bobble. The boy took it and thanked her.

'I must be away now to fetch the baits.' Alec unhooked his bag from the back of the door, and they went out towards the house. Startled hens scattered from the doorstep. 'I won't be long now.'

'Come into the kitchen, Seumas, why don't you, while himself is out there looking for what he's lost, as usual.' The house was modern, and square, with a sloping asbestos roof; Christina's kitchen was bright and tidy, with linoleum on the floor and a heavy cooker against one wall.

'And how are you liking our island?' she asked, loading a plate with cakes. James told her the things he had done since they arrived; but she did not appear to be listening very closely as she busied herself.

'Oh, and that's lovely,' said Christina in her guttural accent. She had a way of speaking as she was drawing in her breath.

He sat and drank his milk, listening to the peeping of the chickens.

When Alec returned there was someone with him, a darker, wind-dried man in his fifties, sporting a white canvas cap. He greeted Christina, and sat down immediately without being invited.

'Found him creeping along the road in his ancient truck,' Alec said, 'searching for a new cow, I'm thinking, now that Catriona is dead.' Although James was not introduced by name, the islanders were speaking in English out of respect for his presence.

'Oh, terrible,' agreed Christina. 'Did you hear what happened?' she asked the boy, who shook his head. 'The Star's cow died yesterday in the evening. Into the early hours they all were, digging a grave for her to be buried in. Just look at the tiredness on them both.' Her voice was shaded with sarcasm.

'You may laugh,' said the other man morosely.

'It's not me that is laughing. But for a man that's back from a cow's funeral, sure Alec was in a fine cheerful mood when he returned.'

'She was a good animal. But we'd to bury her quickly, with the weather.'

Christina had the two men subdued. 'Do you not recognise Calum Angus?' she enquired of the boy. 'He's known on the island as the Star, right enough. Did you never see the film *Whisky Galore?*'

James did not know what she was talking about; it seemed unlikely that the weathered man hunched over his mug of tea was some kind of actor. The Star looked glumly at the table-cloth.

She sucked in a loud breath like someone about to dive. 'Well, he's maybe not in the mood to tell, but on the island of Barra, when the film people arrived, in nineteen forty-eight, it was Calum Angus they chose for a speaking part in the story. That was before he saw the light, right enough.'

'An island of Catholics,' confided Alec, pronouncing the word with three syllables. 'But he changed when he moved over here, to marry Flora. Isn't that so?' He smacked the man's upper arm with the back of his hand.

'Aye, that's it,' said the Star, smiling reluctantly. 'I'm a white settler, no mistake.'

'A foreigner,' agreed Alec. And the men started shaking with laughter, slapping their knees.

'Goodbye,' James said, as they got up. 'Thank you very much for my hat.'

The estate's launch, *Kilbride II*, was moored in the deep bay by the house. Alec had loaded the rods and hand-lines into the little covered cabin, and they headed out to sea, water thumping on the hull. As soon as they had rounded the headland and the house was out of sight, Alec produced a bottle of beer and drank the contents without taking its neck from his lips. He slung it over the side. There was a wooden fish-box positioned over the engine's housing, with a thin-bladed gutting knife stuck into it.

'We've to fill that with cod, or not come home,' the man grinned. He seemed much happier now they were away from the land, a cigarette cocked in his mouth.

With only a slight breeze playing, the sea looked glutinous

and dull. An occasional stronger current of wind would blow a face upon the wrinkled skin of the water, but the motion of the boat, when Alec killed the engine, was scarcely more than a gentle tilting.

He showed the boy how to operate the hand-line, unwinding the thick cuttyhunk cord from its wooden frame, letting down the six feathery lures and their gnarled sinker.

'When you feel the bottom, look, take up three turns, and pull the line against the swell. Then we'll be hauling them in.'

They drifted for ten minutes without speaking, while Alec heaved up and down on his green-heart rod, which was baited with herring.

'Mr Grant told my father the cod had all disappeared.'

'Sure, he knows a lot, that one, for a man who's been here six years.' Alec pressed his lips together, and continued jerking.

'He said the shoals weren't coming this far north.'

'And he's a champion shot when there's no gun to be found, that's certain.'

'I've got one. I've got one.' The boy stripped up his line quickly, feeling the kick of a fish's resistance. He peered excitedly over the side, as a phosphorescent twist came hauling up into view.

'*An dallag*,' pronounced Alec, as the fish landed on the deck. James looked triumphant. 'Spotted dogfish,' the man said. He put the boot of his wader over it, and wrenched the hook free. 'Useless.'

James watched him sling the brown fish overboard. 'Useless for eating,' repeated Alec, 'useless for anything.' They continued fishing, the boy nursing his disappointment. It was the first fish he had ever caught. The dogfish wobbled along the surface on its side, its underslung mouth working slightly, and then it dipped below a wave. 'Don't be worrying,' the man reassured him, 'we'll find your cod for you soon enough.'

They saw no other boats, and the boy began to suspect they were in a hopeless place. After half an hour's effort, they had caught just one fish, and even that had been dismissed; he began to have doubts, recalling, even against his will, the criticisms he had overheard about Alec. But the man continued jagging his rod with an air of confidence, as the launch slid sideways along the indented coastline. Quite suddenly, they both hit fish, deep down. When James pulled up his hand-line there were three mackerel struggling on the end; their tails drummed briskly against the deck as he circled them, wary of the tangled tackle that had collapsed amongst them. Alec was too busy to come to his aid; the rod was hooped and creaking as he tried to drag the tip upright to take the strain. He ordered the boy to fetch the gaff which lay along the boards, its sharpened point masked with a wine-cork.

A bulbous-headed fish thrashed as Alec winched it towards the boat. 'You hold the rod, whilst I cleek him,' he said. The sheer lugging power of cod made the boy's shoulders ache immediately, but he was desperate not to let the prize escape. He pressed the rubber butt of the rod into his abdomen and pulled grimly against the fish.

'The bait,' he cried, 'I can see it – it's coming out. Quick!' Alec was at his side, uncorking his weapon. 'That's never the bait,' he said. 'That's the stomach, popped out wi' the change in the pressure. He'll no swim away from us now.' The cod opened its huge bugle-mouth, crammed with its own guts; it planed feebly in towards the boat, and Alec struck the gaff into its side and as he swung it inboard they heard a sound like a shrill yelp from its congested mouth.

'Nine, maybe ten pounds. There's the boy.' He clubbed the fish between its two protuberant eyes, using the wooden handle of the deck-brush. Alec stuck a thumb through the livid gills, and hoisted it proudly against the backdrop of the waves. A worm-like coil of slime dribbled from its vent.

'Why did it make that funny noise?' James asked him.

'Ach, that was only air,' replied Alec. 'Common enough when you wind them up as fast as I do, boy.' He winked at James, but there was an uneasy look on his face.

At lunch-time they ran the boat ashore and covered the fish-box with kelp, since the rocks offered no shade. They had kept five cod and ten mackerel, their taut brightness clouded in death. Alec was in a mood to relax. From the gas-mask bag that held his midday meal he first produced a half-bottle of whisky. 'Health to men, and death to fish,' he toasted, handing the bottle to James. The boy laughed in embarrassment, and gave it back, unwilling to be left holding it in case there was some kind of ritual attached, like the business with the port.

'What better way to spend a day?' asked the man. It was the first time James had seen him shine so from enjoyment. 'And the sea not being the miser, for once. I tell you, big fellow: we're in the luck.'

'I can't wait to tell them about my cod. And the mackerel.'

'Aye,' Alec grunted, 'they'll no have a lot to show for a day spent driving the roads, by comparison.'

'My father said he was worried about his suspension. We've got to go up to Stornoway on Saturday to collect someone.'

'Mrs Walker, would that be?'

'Yes.'

'That Healey can manage the roads, never mind. It's plenty wide on the way north, and none too many holes. When I was a boy, look, it was faster to go through the hills on foot, up the drove road. Certain things may have improved.'

'Is it true, what they said? That there used to be hundreds more people living here?'

The man hesitated, as he picked the peel off an orange. He sighed, though smiling, and dropped his head. 'Thousands. And not just families gone – whole townships. It was partly the war – two wars, right enough – and since then . . .' He opened his palm and flipped the fruit into it. 'Not a job to be had in the entire place. If I left Graeval, I'd starve. Near enough.' He offered the boy two segments of orange, with a wink.

'But it's a big place,' said James.

'Aye, plenty room and plenty ruins. In Carradale, now, where the herring were good, they'd to leave their houses two years back, for there wasn't the able-bodied men in the place to launch a single boat. Gone to the mainland, the rest of them; Glasgow, or Aberdeen. They come back when the weather's fine, right enough, tourists to a man, saying they've the longing to return here. But Carradale – that place is dead for ever.'

'I'd love to live here, one day.' The boy had an image of the long skies, and the wash of water behind everything. Sitting there in the comfort of the shore, the island seemed to him a place where memory was fresh and short, a wide map of contentment.

Alec seemed unimpressed. 'There was a man who thought that, before the war, *Bodach an t–siabainn*, the wee soapman; Lord Leverhulme, his name was, and mighty fine his ideas were for the life of the place. But he died, and it all came to nothing, as usual.' He was staring at the horizon. 'His trouble was, he was fond of the dancing. The Church didna' approve. And they say he was that deaf he'd carry straight on, though the music of the band had finished.'

He heaved himself up and limped a few yards away from where they had been sitting. His back turned, he released an arc of dark yellow urine on to the cracked soil. 'And now that I've eaten my orange, and squeezed the lemon, we've some fish to kill.'

The boy got up and followed him silently to the launch, the sea beyond them bent like a dented shield.

· · · · ·

He stood clutching the string of fish, about to knock again. 'Miss Mackenzie?' he called through the doorway.

'There's no Miss Mackenzie at home; only Rachel,' came the soft reply from the kitchen, 'so come in, Seumas, and mind that's to be my name when you're visiting, or I'll be calling you Mister Benson, so I will.'

'Alec dropped me off; we've brought you some cod. He said you don't like mackerel.'

She reached for an oval plate standing on the dresser. 'That's kind. There's good meat on the cod, and the heads will be fine baked. Will you fit them on here?'

'I hope I haven't disturbed you.' She was wearing her spectacles, and there was a large book on the table, covered in hairy skin.

'Not at all; you're always welcome indeed.' The woman drew back a chair for him, and made her way to the fireplace for the inevitable kettle.

'I'm afraid I shall have to get back soon. To the lodge, I mean.' James rather hoped she might not assemble another full meal for him, but he was aware that now he was seated, there would be no easy excuse.

Rachel Mackenzie smiled broadly at him, the texture of her skin like unpolished wood. 'Ah. And what business have you, Seumas *ban*, that is so urgent on your young time?'

He blushed, unable to think quickly enough. 'Well . . . nothing, really.'

'Well, take care, for if you spend long doing nothing, the idle-worms will grow on your fingers, sure as rain.' She wriggled a hand in the air, dissolving his embarrassment with her laugh. 'You've the reading of books to attend to, would that be it? As you were telling me.' He nodded, grateful for the excuse she was offering on his behalf. She began to ask him about his school, and whether he was happy there. James said it was all right, but of course he preferred being at home, though as he said that he wondered if it was strictly true.

'I've got lots of friends there,' he told her, 'and it's quite good fun.'

Miss Mackenzie nodded, stirring the leaves in the pot. 'And the red-haired boy, would he be one of your friends?'

He looked back at her puzzled. He could not remember mentioning anything about Guy Walker.

'Aye, well, you were telling me of him when first you

were here,' she went on. 'And I minded it, for the ruddy hair is a rare thing on this island. There's not many born with it. Indeed, there hasn't been a marriage in these parts for a year now anyway.'

'Yes,' said James, 'one of them has got red hair.'

She brought the pot to the table, and set it down between them. 'Now, if it's books you like, would you care to take a look into mine there, while that's making?' she said. 'It's a grand book, that, the best that I have, and an old one, too. *Gras am Pailteas*: the *Grace Abounding* of John Bunyan, though this is in the Gaelic, so you'll not be understanding many of the words.'

'I've never heard of that one.'

'There's many a copy kept in the home on these islands; and the Bible, too, of course. I can still make out the words fair enough, even with these eyes, for it has the large print.' She opened the supple cover. 'In the first page there you can see inscribed the names of every person born to the Mackenzie family on this island for one hundred and fifty years past. Their names are written in there at birth, by the oldest of the living relations.'

James looked at the neat procession of entries, each one bearing several Christian names. 'Is one of these you?'

'There I am, look. In eighteen-seventy I first greeted the sun, born right here on the bay.'

'What, in this house?'

'No, no. My nephew built this with his friends. Since the war.' She pointed to the door. 'Out there, was our home.'

He looked at her in disbelief. 'In the shed?'

'*Tigh dubh, tigh dubh*,' she corrected him. 'That was no a shed in those days. A black house, it was called; not very modern. We'd the fire in the centre, and the cattle away to one end, for the warmth. Yes indeed, all of us in there together, when I was born. And a large family it was, for a time, though I shall be the last, for Alec has not a family and he was my sister Peigi's only child.'

67

Rachel Mackenzie ran her nail under the names on the list. 'My mother, now, *bean-ghluin* she was, the knee-woman; like a midwife, and a mourning-woman together. There at the beginning and the end, up and down these bays. Three drops of water for the new child, to sign the Trinity, as Bride did to her foster-son, and at the end the eyes closed, and a plate of salt. But the sadness of it was, so many never survived the bed of their birth, for the rose.'

'What do you mean?' The boy was shaken by this abrupt flow of memory.

'Wildfire. A terrible catching thing it was, with burning marks on the body; and in a nursing mother, like a rose glowing on the breast. A baby would die from the milk, and never a cure for it. It was a terrible thing, in those days, to see the children dying, but there was not the medicine to help us, except the *brochan* for a cough.'

She poured tea into two cups. Her hands looked strong, with their greenish roots of blood. James listened to her voice continue in its wavering rhythm.

'The large grey seal, now, *ron mor*, he had the oil that we used when a person had sickened. The fat could be boiled down until it was clear, and that was feeding. So every year the men would take to the boats, and row with their sweeps out to the skerries where there were colonies of these seals. Awful strong is the big seal, but his strength passes into the oil. If he caught a leg in his jaws, he would bite through to the bone before ever he'd let you go, and they would put charcoal in their leggings, so the seal would think he'd the bone broken at once, from the sound.'

The boy was spellbound. 'It must have been awfully dangerous,' he said. It was like the stories he'd read of men in the swamps fighting crocodiles.

'So it was,' she replied. '*Ola-an-roin* was all that we had for the white scourge, the tuber-culosis, as it is known. Five families there were living on this bay when I was a girl, and each with some person suffering.' Once again, her finger went to the book.

'And the youngest that survived of our family was John, my brother. He was a strong man, right enough. Many's the time I carried him on my back into yon bay where the boat would be waiting, so he'd not start the night with his feet soaking cold. It was not just the children that the island women bore. And at next light he'd be home, often enough his face and arms ribboned red from the scalders, the jellyfish they shook from their ropes in the dark. With him smiling, and wanting his meal.'

James tinkered with his cup and saucer. The old woman was leaning forward in her chair, tugging the shawl more tightly around her shoulders. He did not feel he should interrupt her reverie.

'When the fishings were good, mind, the men would be away for days on end, and often at the worst times for us. Ploughing or harvest, with just the old ones to help.' She chuckled. 'You'd not get much work out of the likes of myself at the foot-plough, or digging the thatch into the lazy-beds. Many there were took to the ships and emigrated: to the cold country, *an talamh fuar*, to Canada. And that was as well, for there was here no living to be had, and the soil in places that shallow you could never even bury the dead.'

Rachel Mackenzie sat in her shawl next to the fire and shivered.

'You must forgive me,' she said. 'These things are past, but not forgotten in this house. A scar will ache in warm weather.'

'Did your brother go to Canada as well?' he asked politely.

She put down the teapot very slowly. 'He did not. *Chaochail e*: he changed, that's what we would say when the sea took a person from us. In the second hour of the first day of nineteen-hundred-and-nineteen, it was, and he coming back with the others from the war. He had been fighting in the trenches, and a wonder it was that he was still alive. *Foghar nam ban breidgheal* — that harvest of young widows. The boat that they took from the mainland was named the *Iolaire*, and as she entered the harbour she was moving too fast; she struck on the rocks, the Beasts of Holm, and they went down into the night of that winter water, and us there in the darkness waiting. Two hundred and five men taken, with the bodies washed up in the harbour after dawn, drifting with the packages they had brought home to the island for us. John they could not find, but the body of the Captain was discovered, with two of the lifebelts around him.'

The boy saw a remote look in her eyes as she imagined the scene.

'I'm sorry,' he mouthed.

The woman shook her head. 'Well, no. It's parting with the living that makes the sorest wound, and it's no sense grieving for the dead, and drowning them twice. There were few men hereabouts met their death on a pillow: the sea searches for her own.'

She seemed to be looking through him, focusing on something distant. Her words came more slowly. 'And later that night, for the first time in the memory of the living, a winter sky was filled with the Northern Streamers – *na fir chlis*, the quick men, the dancers. Some call them the Northern Lights; they have many names. Leaping over our sorrow they went, green and white and red were their shafts, shaking their spearlight away across the horizon. It showed us a comfort. It reminded us where they had gone.'

The boy was suddenly frightened. Her reminiscences had cast a chill over his impression of the landscape; for the first time he could picture the loneliness of the shoreline, the hardness of the rocks. It was perhaps not as he had imagined. Flames flapped in the grate as she stoked the fire, and James glanced around her room, taking in its lack of comforts. He could see now it might not be such a good place to live alone.

Perhaps she sensed his anxiety. '*Bha la eile ann,*' she said, her voice burring at its normal speed, 'that was another time, and the memory of it is keen only to myself. You must understand, Seumas *ban*, that there are many moods to the ocean;

70

she must be loved amid our fear, for there is fruitfulness as well as danger. My father, now, didn't he teach me to taste the wind for the scent of scales in it, when a grand catch would be made, and how to name the tides that would bring the harvest of kelp, or the shoals of glittering herrings. If you learn such things, she may not harm you.' James was staring deep into her clear eyes.

'The sea is an old woman,' she said, 'older even than myself. With jealousy she'll guard what is hers, and there are times in her laughing mood when the waves leap from the rocks, and every fang is showing. That's the day to be by a fire and ignore her. But go to the great beach by night, to *traigh mhor* where the eel swims and the cattle walked out of the water, and it's there that the nightwind murmurs through the marram grass, and the waves stroke the white shore with their noise, and are gentle. *Ceol na mara*, we call it, the sea music, and it is the soft sound that fills the dark, the ebb and the flow; the sea breathing with her breath, but there's few will stop and listen.'

James felt lulled by the lilt of her voice. He cradled the warm cup in his hands, and thought of the place she described, where he had discovered his secret hollow in the dunes.

'I saw the house there,' he told her. 'There was a boy outside it.'

Miss Mackenzie smiled distantly at him, shaking her head. 'No, that is some other place. No one lives by there now,' she told him gently. 'They are all gone.'

'The other day,' he insisted. 'I didn't speak to him, because I was looking for someone else.' Maybe he had been dreaming, after all.

'You've a way to walk,' said Miss Mackenzie, suddenly standing. 'I should not make you linger. Or night the herdsman will be bringing all home, and you not yet at the lodge.' The low sound of her chair roused him, and he stood up at once. 'I thank you for the fish,' she said, 'and for your coming.'

71

'I'll tell Dr Willis about the seal oil,' he said. 'I'll bet he'll be interested in that.'

'Ah well,' she cautioned him, 'maybe it would be best if you didn't tell them at all you were calling on me.' She leaned thoughtfully against the back of her chair.

'But why?' he asked. 'Is something wrong?'

'No, no. Never a thing. But it might not seem proper for a young gentleman from the lodge to be wasting his time so. Especially when you've the studying to do.' She smiled slowly at him. 'It could be like a secret,' she said.

James liked the idea of that, and he agreed. When he reached the point of the headland, he looked back, expecting her to be standing by the door, but she was not. He jumped from the rocks on to the sand, the light lifting over a bent and cobbled world.

VIII

'I'm mighty sorry to be disturbing you, sir,' intoned Grant, standing stiffly in the hallway, hat in hand. It was the morning before they were due to meet the ferry.

'Perfectly all right. What can I do for you?' replied Benson, dabbing egg from the side of his mouth as he came from the dining-room. 'Another bloody hot day, that's for sure.' They went into the little office by the foot of the staircase.

'Do sit.' The room was not often used, and smelt fusty. There was a faded blind pulled down over the single window, and Benson switched on the light, its glass bowl sprinkled with the summer harvest of dead insects.

'In a way, it's about the weather that I've come, Mr Benson. Two months now without a drop o' sky water, and no change coming that I can see. It's the salmon in the estuary, sir. They're awful vulnerable.'

'So I imagine.' He unstrapped his wristwatch and began winding it.

The keeper leaned forward on the desk. 'It's no so much the local boys – we've patrols, and that, at night and they know what's what. But there is the seals. Only this morning I'm seeing one at the mouth of the Mircavat river here, and that's never the first time, either.'

'What can you do?'

'To shoot one would be the thing.'

Benson looked at him quizzically. 'Is that the standard practice?'

'Aye, well, from time to time. Yon selchies seat an awful big dinner.'

'Surely you don't need my permission, though?'

'It's the ammunition, sir. Mr Kershaw requires an inventory. If you're agreeable.'

'Yes, I suppose so,' said Benson. 'But, look; I'd be grateful if you could take care of this business without upsetting the ladies. You know. Pick a time when they're out driving, or something, could you? They might not understand. Are you with me?'

Grant nodded sagaciously. 'In fact, sir, I was going to suggest Campbell for the job. He could attend to it tomorrow, and he's maybe the better shot with a rifle, I don't mind saying. They're canny buggers, the selchies – pardon the expression sir – and it will take a man the best part of a day to get close. I've to be in town in the morning for the fuel-drums.'

The men stood up simultaneously. 'Very well. See to it, then.'

Willie Grant touched his forehead. 'I will, Mr Benson. It'll be a pleasure.'

. . . . .

As he slid across the seat of the Healey James already felt hot in his flannel shirt and tweed jacket. The interior of the car smelt heady with leather, and he wound down the window as he waited. He looked at the map his father had given him, the coastal road to the north marked over in red crayon; the villages through which they had to pass bore long, unpronounceable Gaelic names, and he hoped he would not have to navigate much during the journey.

'Ready?' asked Benson, bundling his blazer on to the back seat. 'All set?' He tucked a clutch of letters into the dashboard. The boy smiled in affirmation. He loved being driven in his father's new car, and he longed to see this other part of the island, where Alec had told him the people were small and dirty.

'Yes,' he replied. 'Are we off?'

The car swung round the cobblestones, and hissed towards

74

the drive. Just then, Alec appeared at the door of the tackle-room with a small carton in his hand. He seemed not to notice the boy's wave, but stood gazing seriously at the sky. Despite the heat, a long storm-cape hung over his shoulder. Although the drive took them more than two hours, his father seemed less impatient than usual. There was something languid in his manner as he steered, one elbow on the sill of the open window, his shirt-sleeves rolled up. 'Wouldn't fancy doing this trip at night,' he said, as they swung to avoid pitted areas in the road. 'Fat lot of good the local council has done in this part of Scotland, I'm sure.'

They passed few other cars, and most of the traffic consisted of haulage lorries whose slow progress occupied the whole width of the road. To overtake, his father pressed the horn once and they pulled in at the next passing-place with a toot-toot of greeting. It was like taking part in some relay race.

To their right, the coast was indented with a series of thin fiord-like sea-lochs, with a sparse scattering of crofts along the water's edge where shelter and safe anchorage were afforded. There was no vista of the open sea such as the lodge enjoyed, and the bouldery land-mass began to disappear; the terrain flattened and gave way to peat-bogs stretching away to their left, yellow and sour, interrupted only by banks of cut moss and the numerous dark discs of water, where the little meniscus of each lochan was shivering in the breeze and the sun.

James imagined the landscape rolling up like a huge carpet behind them as they passed.

As they motored through the small townships, the low houses all built along the road, his father had to reduce speed drastically because of the packs of dogs that gathered around the car, yowling and snapping at the wheels. 'Sunny Siberia, complete with wolves,' he said.

'It does look rather like a desert,' observed James.

Benson leaned on the horn. 'If one of those mongrels so

75

much as touches my paintwork, he's for it.' He changed down and revved his engine in a useless attempt to scatter them.

A girl with long hair was staring at them silently over her gate.

. . . . .

With the massive rifle slung diagonally across his back, Alec made his way slowly along the shoreline towards the Mircavat estuary. There was scarcely a breeze to move the grasses, and the greenish sea was lifting gently. He was wearing a khaki shirt and a pair of army fatigues, and carried the gas-mask bag containing his lunch. Where the thin river washed feebly into the angle of the bay he set down his equipment on the rocks and folded the cape into a bundle as a rest for his elbows, his movements mechanical and without eagerness.

Although the tide was already on the turn, it would be an hour at least before it bore the shoals of fish close enough into the shore for him to observe them clearly, and there was nothing for him to do but wait. He placed his bag and field-glasses in a crevice by the cape and tore open the carton of long bullets.

He withdrew a bottle from the bag and twisted it down into the cool sand of the river bed. His palate felt furry with thirst, and he scooped a smooth pebble out of the fresh water and popped it into his mouth, sucking for the moisture. There would be time for two cigarettes before any danger of scaring off his quarry. Alec stretched on his back and felt the comfort of the hard rock straightening his body.

. . . . .

Even in the main street of the town sheep rocked their way across the path of the traffic in a silly gallop. The windows of the little shops displayed a jumble of mixed wares – rope, tinned food, postcards, knitwear – and there were few pedestrians to be seen. They parked the car by the pier-head and his father went into the ticket-office to check whether the ferry was on time. The window was open, but there was no one behind it.

'How absolutely typical,' he said.

There were several trawlers tied up in the harbour and from one the catch was being unloaded by a bearded young man operating a derrick. The bagnet of fish was hoisted aloft from the hold and swung, dripping slightly, over the waiting containers where it shed its streaming load with a sudden rumble of slapping. A collie trotted out of the wheel-house and stood, ears cocked, a mackerel in its jaws.

'I gather there is one hotel that is not entirely unsalubrious,' said Benson, hooking the blazer over his shoulder with one finger. 'Shall we spy out the land? I think a gin and tonic is indicated.'

'Do you want the letters?' asked the boy.

'Yes, of course. See if you can find a pillar-box.'

Despite the monochrome faces of the greystone buildings, the water-front had a Mediterranean stillness in the midday heat. James had never before seen a port like this; it was unlike the seaside places he had visited, with their beach balls and spades and the bright paraphernalia of southern recreation. The uninterrupted facade of Victorian buildings, with rusty streaks where pipes spouted rainwater most of the year, looked closed and abandoned. Seamen's Union, Co-operative Association, Trawler Bar, read the small signs by the doors.

A man in overalls stepped carefully out of a doorway, cupping a cigarette in the palm of his hand. 'Hang on, I'll ask this chap the way,' said Benson to the boy. The seaman leaned heavily on his shoulder and began pointing vaguely down the water-front. He raised his hand to them as they walked off, and stood frozen in the posture until his arm seemed to drop of its own accord. He continued gazing after them as they entered the chipped porch of the Royal Highland Hotel above which a Union Jack hung slackly.

'We wanted some lunch,' said his father, looking into the bar. 'Are you open?'

'Surely,' replied the man behind the counter, arranging glasses methodically on a shelf. There was no one else in the small room, and the low tables were stacked with upturned stools. 'I shall be with you gentlemen in just a moment, now.' He shrugged on a plum-coloured jacket and crossed to where they were seated under the bevelled glass window. Nodding to them, he presented a dog-eared menu-card in a bright blue folder draped with tassels. He began to wipe the still damp surface of their table.

Benson asked James what he wanted, and ordered the drinks. The man withdrew without speaking. 'Well, I'll be damned,' he snorted. '"A member of the Gordon Highlander Group of Hotels"; one of Charlie Russell's chain. This place!' He clicked his tongue in amazement.

'It isn't very busy,' said the boy, 'considering how hot every-one must be.' He perched on the banquette and sipped his warm lemonade through a paper straw. 'It's completely empty.'

'I think you will find there are a number of rival establish-ments for the locals to slake their thirsts in, without paying these prices,' his father said. 'Charlie Russell. Well, I'm damned.' A faint buzz came from his glass as he raised it to his mouth.

In the flock-papered dining-room only two other tables were occupied. A man in a tweed suit sat alone at one, con-centrating on a bowl of yellowish soup, while in the middle of the room a young couple were self-consciously bending to their stew, two travelling-bags at their feet. The busy silence was punctuated only by the thin scraping of cutlery against ceramic dishware.

His father consulted his watch. 'Forty minutes at least until she docks, assuming some kind of observance of the published timetables.' He turned over the little shape of pressed pâté on its singed-looking lettuce leaf as if expecting to see something crawl out from beneath it. 'Hungry?' he asked the boy. James said yes, he was, and spooned the maraschino cherry from the centre of his melon-cube cocktail, where it left a pucker of pink.

'I trust you have enjoyed yourself,' Benson began suddenly, his cheek padded with pâté. He transferred the desiccated mass across his palate and took a quick gulp of water. 'You seem to have found plenty to entertain you.'

'It's been jolly good fun,' said James politely. 'It's a very nice place, the island.'

The man continued to churn his mouthful. 'Well, I'm glad. There have been times when I've been worried about your being, you know,' he raised his knife like the indicator of an automobile, 'at a loose end. You really must come out to the lochs next week. Monday, say; and see what it's all about.'

'Yes, I would like to try.'

'Good egg.' Two plates of liver and onions arrived, and a bottle of wine in a sloping wickerwork container.

'Try a little wine? Why not; won't do you any harm.' He splashed some into the boy's tumbler and motioned to him to add water. 'By the way, Mrs Paton is very pleased with the shells you've been finding for her. Going to decorate some boxes with them, or something. Well done.' He pursed his lips at him and nodded. James felt warm with this unaccustomed approval.

It had been Dr Willis's idea that he bring back a few more shells whenever he went out near the beaches, and the woman had looked startled at the gesture at first, then nervously grateful. She had scraped the offerings from the pail with the cupped claws of her hand and turned away at once, back to the card-table in the corner where she had set up her little factory with tweezers and glue.

His father extracted a piece of tubular gristle from his mouth, and flicked it on to the plate. He began mopping up gravy with his bread. 'What do you think of the plan to take the lodge next year, every year even? As you get older, you can get to know the place really well, we might even try and buy it. Continuity is a good thing, you know – the basis of all security.' He had assumed his boardroom manner. 'Why, this time next year you'll be about to go to Harrow. You're growing up. We have to think of that, eh?'

The boy looked into his tumbler. Its faint antiseptic smell reminded him of the school corridors.

. . . . .

Just as he was biting into the fleecy white sandwich he became aware of a commotion away to his left. Alec rolled over into position by his cape, and saw a mottled grey shape bob above the waves, followed by an undulating body that sounded at once in a flap of spray. He snapped forward the bolt on his rifle.

The shoal of salmon was some fifty yards from the mouth of the river in front of him. He could make out the odd tail fidgeting along the surface, but they showed no signs of agitation. The only indication of their mass below the water was the almost imperceptible way the waves washed with a faint bulge over their packed numbers. Alec concentrated on the cleft of sea in his sights; there would be one chance only for a clear shot when the seal appeared again before feeding, and if he missed he would not see it again. He knew how wary they were: for months after, that seal would only go foraging at night, once it knew danger.

A solitary fulmar slid along the bright curve of the afternoon.

. . . . .

He tipped some of the pale carmine liquid into his mouth, held it for a second, and swallowed.

'There, how's that? Good for the circulation.' His father raised his own glass and mimed a toast. 'Like it?'

'Not really,' he answered truthfully, replacing his tumbler on the cloth.

Benson looked disappointed. He began to slice his shrivelled cheese into cubes.

'Soon make a man of you,' he said. 'Wine today, the world tomorrow; as the saying is.' His eyes had assumed a pearly gleam.

When they had finished eating, his father lit a cigar and pushed his chair back sharply. He stretched luxuriously and looked around the room. 'Not such a bad place, after all, considering where it is,' he murmured through the smoke. James folded his napkin and sat still. The couple at the centre table were poring over their bill, picking their way through a little pile of coins on the plate.

Benson stretched forward across the table, pinching a thread of tobacco off his tongue with his other hand. 'Well, if you're not going to finish it, I suppose I'd better,' he said, reaching for James's abandoned wine. The boy's hand, eager to assist, instinctively moved to lift it towards his father, and the glass toppled over with a dull crack.

'Why did God make you so clumsy?' asked Richard Benson, his eyelids drooping in exasperation as he watched the stain blossoming into the cloth.

. . . . .

The head emerged suddenly, and the sleek lines of the neck and body followed until the seal was reared partly out of the water, leaning slightly backwards against the force of its tail. The whiskered face calmly surveyed the surface of the waves, and the fish plunging nearby.

Alec swung his shoulders in a reflex, gauging the distance. The foresight lined up between the arms of the vee and he pulled the butt hard into his shoulder as he squeezed.

The seal reeled sideways and dived. He stood up at once and reloaded, as the sky rolled to the echo of the report and the shoreline exploded with screaming white birds, dashing out along the water and banking steeply as they crossed the headland where he was now moving. He was unsure if his shot had gone home, for the creased water where the seal had disappeared looked deserted and clean.

Binoculars flapping against his chest, he struggled down on to the beach, crossed the narrow river, and began to run along the sand towards the left-hand arm of the bay. Oblivious to the squalling sky he scanned the sliding waves for some indication that he had hit his mark, but no long grey carcass floated into view on the back of the tide. Reaching the promontory that divided the bay from the sea in front of the lodge he heaved his bad leg up the rocks and dropped on to one knee, fighting to control his breathing. It had been a long time since Alec had attempted to run.

After five minutes a long nose slid noiselessly above the sea in front of Graeval Lodge as the creature surfaced for air. From where he was positioned, it was a difficult shot but Alec fired immediately, and this time there was a small spurt of blood as the bullet passed through its lower jaw, and the seal swivelled several times violently in the water. He sent another shot into its flank, above the forward flipper, and then the entire body began floating like a volcanic pumice-stone on the tide.

Rosemary Cooper laid down her dessert spoon. 'What on earth is all that noise?' she exclaimed.

'I expect it's the men,' said Alice, prising the lid off a tin, 'fooling around with their guns.' She unwound a spoonful of treacle down into her milk pudding.

. . . . .

'Richard, cooee!' She stood by the rail, waving dramatically.

'There she is,' his father said, pushing himself away from the bonnet where he was leaning. He left the boy standing by the car as he strode forwards.

Venetia Walker advanced down the gangplank clutching a Vuitton travel-bag. 'Richard. Darling.' She presented to him a powdery cheek.

He smiled into her face. 'How was the crossing?'

'Perfect,' she said. 'I read a divine book.' She allowed herself to be steered towards the Healey, his hand in the small of her back.

'Jamie. How lovely this is.' She kissed him on the forehead with an accompanying hum of affection. Over her arm was a smart camel-hair coat.

'But I tell you, Richard,' she said, laying a hand on his wrist as if feeling for the pulse, 'I practically died of the heat. What is this place you have summoned me to – the Scotch Riviera?'

The adults laughed. A porter in a blue shirt came up with a large suitcase, a pigskin bag and a varnished wooden box with a handle.

Benson opened the boot. 'What's this?' he asked in dismay.

'You silly man, that's my easel. I never travel without it, you should know that. And now, I'm ready. Take me to your castle.'

As soon as they were on their way she began rummaging in her bag, and finally extracted a glass-stoppered jar which she passed round the seat to the boy sitting in the back.

'I brought these for you,' she said with her curling smile. 'I gather that shops are rather thin on the ground in these parts.' It was a jar of bull's-eyes, with a coloured picture of the Coronation coach on the label.

'Gosh, thanks.' He grasped the glass cylinder and shook it with delight.

'And this. I thought this might come in handy.' She presented him with a clasp-knife, a single slim blade folded into a horn handle. There was a little silver shield inlaid, to take the owner's initials. Mrs Walker skewed around on her seat, one leg tucked under her body. 'Maybe you could carve me something with it?'

He looked at her uncooperatively. 'But there aren't any trees.'

'Oh.' She gave a disconcerted pout. 'Then perhaps some driftwood or something?'

'What do you say, James?' prompted his father.

'Thank you. Thank you very much.' He settled back to examine his two trophies.

They rattled over the cattle-grid that marked where the town was notionally divided from the moorland, and swept left on to the road leading south once again.

'Well, Santa Claus, haven't you got anything for me?' his father asked her. She looked out of her side-window. 'Maybe I have. You'll just have to wait and see,' she said.

Venetia Walker was enthusiastic about everything they passed. Never in her life, she declared, had she seen such sensational countryside. This seemed to amuse James's father until, on the outskirts of one of the thin, linear townships which looked to him identical with all the others, she insisted he stop the car so she could photograph an old man and his untidy dog. She made a certain fuss by trying to explain to the crofter that she wished him to pose in front of a telegraph-pole, to emphasise the connection between old and new. He and his dog complied in an expressionless sort of way, and Mrs Walker looked satisfied, shaking him graciously by the hand when the photography was completed.

'Honestly,' said Benson as they moved off, 'you can be so embarrassing.'

She gave a shrill laugh. 'What could be embarrassing about meeting a nice old man? You're being too ridiculous.'

James had never heard anyone address his father in quite such a way.

'There are endless old people you can photograph to your heart's desire when we get there,' said Benson huffily.

'Oh good. But I wanted to photograph that one.' Her voice ended in a soft gurgle.

His father began to drive faster.

'Anyway,' she concluded, 'what would you know about my heart's desire?'

For some time there was no further conversation. James fixed his attention on the telephone wire that ran along the left side of the road, watching the downward curve as it

84

slackened between poles, then rose as if about to break free, only to be plucked down as the next pole whizzed past. He wondered where it all ended up, disappearing into the side of some box on a building.

'Oh, Jamie, I almost forgot,' she said, swivelling round to face him, ignoring his taciturn father. 'Guy sends his love. He's gone to the Dordogne for his hols. To our villa. He'll be too jealous when he knows what glorious weather we are having up here, don't you think?'

The boy curled up along the seat. He wasn't sure where the Dordogne was exactly, but his mind had an imaginary map of Europe that stretched away south from London, each country coloured differently, with the bulb of Africa just appearing on the horizon. He thought of himself hovering over the blue mass of France, while somewhere below him was Guy Walker crouching by a hot stone wall. He was holding his magnifying-glass, the pocket one he had, with the leather case, and was burning an ant-hill in its beam. He had done that one afternoon while they were lying on their rugs watching the first eleven play cricket, the tiny incinerated bodies budding briefly into flame, one after the other.

'He's such an admirer of Jamie's,' she said to his father, 'he says he's one of the cleverest boys in the entire school.' There was no reply. 'Isn't that wonderful?' she insisted.

For a moment, the uncountable miles that must be between them gave James a thrill of relief. It even seemed possible that he might never have to see Guy Walker again, with his red hair and the sour smell that came off his freckled skin. He imagined the other boy skulking through some French garden, his fists stuck menacingly in the pockets of his shorts.

It was Walker who had started calling him Daphne. Every Thursday night they had to queue on the landing outside the dormitories and deposit their dirty laundry into the big open baskets, and one evening during the Easter term, Walker had retrieved one of James's socks and held it aloft. 'Hey, Benson. What's this?' The front of the name-tape, which Mrs

85

Cassell, their housekeeper, had tucked in, had come unstitched and his mother's Christian name unfurled. His sock was now labelled 'Daphne Benson'. 'Doesn't your mother need name-tapes any more then?' demanded Walker, knowing where she was. 'Eh? Daphne?'

James twisted the stopper from the neck of the jar and put two boiled sweets into his dry mouth.

. . . . .

'It's Campbell, I think. He seems to be fishing.'

'Here, let me look,' said Rosemary, one hand already on the binoculars. 'I thought he was out with the men.'

He had gone for the launch as soon as he was certain it was dead, and now Alec was swinging a grapple on the end of a rope, to haul the seal inboard. He had drawn up the *Kilbride II* between the carcass and the lodge, to disguise his activity as far as was possible, but the tide was now full, and the boat was difficult to manoeuvre single-handed.

'He's got something,' Alice Paton said curiously.

The tines caught in the tough skin, and he pulled. As the seal glided in towards the launch it gave a convulsive sweep of its tail, and he lost his grip on the rope. The animal shuddered, nerves rippling its body, though the deep brown eye never moved. A thick froth bubbled gently from its nostrils. Alec swore, soaked with sweat and spray, as he heaved the enormous corpse into the gunwales and made it fast with a noose around the tail.

'What is it?' asked Rosemary, handing back the glasses.

The other woman focused as Alec turned the launch and towed his burden towards the point. 'I won't look,' she cried, bursting away from the window. 'How could they? How could they do such a thing?' Her body was shivering with alarm as she slid sideways on to a chair.

'Oh yes,' observed Rosemary Cooper. 'I see. It's a seal.'

. . . . .

When he went up to his room to wash before tea, James discovered the letters in the pocket of his jacket. There were five identical envelopes, and he examined each one in turn, unsure of what to do. All but one were addressed in his father's precise handwriting. They had been his responsibility.

He went quickly down the stairs, passing the drawing-room without daring to look in. There was some kind of argument going on, and he heard his father's voice bearing down on the others. James ran along the side of the courtyard, close to the wall, fearful that he might meet the Land Rover arriving back with the party of fishermen, but he made it out under the arch and was soon on the beach.

At first, he was not sure he had found the right place. Behind the dunes was the hollow where he had lain and listened to the wind in the marram-grass, but there was no sign of the little house where he thought he had seen the boy. But he was in a hurry, and dug a furrow with the heel of his sandal, burying the envelopes as deep as he could. Then he climbed back over to the beach, scooped up enough shells to fill one pocket, and ran quickly back to Graeval Lodge, where he would have another bull's-eye after tea.

IX

It was past nine, but he was the only one down and had sat alone at the breakfast table with his tea and plate of toast. As he plodded back upstairs clutching his book there came the leisurely sounds of morning activity from the top floor; the dull pad of footsteps and the rumble of water plunging into a bath. James shone a green apple against his trouser-leg as he climbed.

Sunlight played in slanted squares across the drawing-room carpet. The beige blinds were down, and the air was stale with the lingering smoke of cigars. He went to the bay window and drew down the cord of the central blind: the fabric was old and fly-spotted, with a tawny horizontal stain where it had lodged for years against the wooden roller. He released it with a jerk, and the bobble tapped its way up the glass.

The skin of the fruit was puckered from its journey, and the flesh was woolly and disappointing, but he finished eating it methodically, savouring the delay that this permitted before he must start work. On the cushion of the window-seat lay Kennedy's Latin Primer. It was Mr Luxmoore's own copy, scuffed but unadorned with the usual graffiti of the books issued during term time. James had promised his father he would spend the morning quietly with his book, but the prospect of it made his mind feel dry.

Twirling the core by its stalk, he skimmed it out of the open window towards the sea.

'You're up bright and early, young sir,' said Geoffrey Willis from the doorway. 'Writer's itch, is it? *Furor scribendi?*' James could not be sure if he had caught him. He stood awkwardly, his back to the morning sky with its high shredded clouds. A thick breeze was riffling the water below.

'Lovely smell,' said the doctor, sniffing like an animal. 'Fresh flowers somewhere; must be.' He lowered himself heavily into the wing-backed chair. 'Mind if I join you? Two gentlemen of letters together, in this den of illiteracy.' He raised his eyebrows twice and smiled encouragingly.

James turned over his volume to show the cover. 'I'm doing gender rhymes,' he said.

There was a hissing sound of recognition. 'Don't tell me,' said Willis. He pointed at the ceiling and screwed up his eyes. 'Something about a dormouse – am I right?'

'*Glis*,' replied the boy. He recited the section of the rhyme. '*Sanguis, pulvis, cucumis, Lapis, casses, Manes, glis.*'

'Just so. The long-tailed dormouse, exactly. The Romans used to eat them. Makes you think.' He tugged a book out of his pocket and straightened the dog-eared corner of a page. 'Fancy me remembering the dormouse!' he said delightedly as he settled.

They read on without speaking further, the occasional flourish of breeze stroking the shaved back of the boy's neck as he lay on his stomach under the window. A greenish fly was making a frying noise against the pane. He worked mechanically through the clusters of nouns, rattling a pencil between his teeth. Rather than learn them by rote, he found it better to visualise each one separately as he transcribed it, because that way you could invent little stories to connect the unlikely words.

> Chiefly Masculine we find,
> Sometimes Feminine declined,
> *Callis, sentis, funis, finis*,
> and in poets *torquis, cinis*.

He imagined a man – a Roman pirate, in sandals perhaps – fighting his way along a path thick with thorns. He was clutching an old map. He let himself down on a rope, down an overgrown cliff-face on to a ledge where there was some hidden treasure. The pirate raised a gleaming necklace before his eyes.

The part about the cinders didn't really fit in, though. James bit into the painted hexagon of his pencil-end. It wouldn't work if one of the nouns was missing. Maybe the Mediterranean sun, magnified through one of the sparkling jewels, burned the map to cinders as he gloated, and he never discovered the rest of the hoard. James wondered if there was any treasure lying under the sea around the island. He would ask the old woman when next he saw her, because she seemed to know everything about the place.

In the margin alongside this section of the Third Declension, Mr Luxmoore's pencil had inscribed a single vertical stroke to remark its particular importance.

'Good morning, good morning,' said Willis as the two others entered. 'Sleep well, I hope? Sovereign remedy, nothing wrong in that.'

The boy sat up politely. Michael Cooper craned over the doctor's shoulder and pointed at his book. 'What's all this, Geoffrey? Not brushing up on your medicine, surely?'

Willis chuckled defensively. 'Heavens, no; never fear. Just a spot of light relief.' He yielded the book reluctantly.

'Ernest Hemingway. Well. Any good?'

'Gripping stuff, definitely.' Willis tapped the open page in recommendation. 'All about a Spanish chappie latching into a whopper. I shall lend it to you once I'm through.' Firmly, he recovered his novel.

Paton looked at him distantly. He appeared to be thinking of something else. 'An American book. I see.'

'You'll be drinking cocktails next, and practising with a drawl,' said Cooper.

'Ha, ha,' went Willis. 'I think not, Michael.'

Alvus, Arctus, carbasus . . . the boy persisted with the rhythm of his exercise. He would have to face a test on all of this when he got back.

'Seen the papers?' Cooper frowned around the room.

'Fattish chance of any today,' said the doctor to his book.

'No, no. Venetia brought up a bunch from London yesterday. I bet Richard has snaffled them.'

'That would come as no surprise.' Bobby Paton's voice was rigid with sarcasm. He was standing in front of the fire-screen, twirling the signet ring around his little finger.

Neuter *pelagus* and *virus*;
Vulgus Neuter commonly . . .

He forced his concentration upon the individual words, excluding the unpleasant tone he felt vibrating from the adult conversation.

'What's that, Bobby; something wrong?'

Paton sent a fist into his palm. 'What do you think?'

He struggled to keep the picture in his imagination. A fat white bear was spinning cloth under a dark cluster of vine leaves. In the background he thought up an orchard of pears.

'Not now, Bobby. You know?' Cooper nodded his head towards the window-seat. 'Not just now.'

Studiously persisting with his novel, Dr Willis cleared his throat uneasily as he turned crisply between pages. Paton was scratching his cuff and wriggling his wrist as if disengaging it from some obstacle. 'I believe my wife is entitled to an apology. He should have consulted us. He knows perfectly well about Alice.'

'It went wrong, that's all. Let me see what I can do.'

'But not him. Snowball's chance in hell.'

'Leave it to me.'

Bobby Paton suddenly stamped his foot on the rug. He stared fixedly at it as if paralysed. 'It isn't bloody good enough.' He began to gasp, thin-lipped, like a fish. 'I simply will not see her reduced to this again. And bugger the niceties of the situation.' He stepped forward defiantly, glaring at the boy. 'I want this thing out in the open.'

Aequor, marmor, cor decline
Neuter; *arbor* feminine.

His cheeks pulsed, he forced himself to read the words in his head.

There was a curious tingling between his shoulder-blades and he began to feel terribly hot.

'Bobby. The very man I was looking for,' said his father, sauntering into the room in his long dressing-gown. 'Have you a moment?'

. . . . .

Later, he went down into the garden to escape the distractions. He sat on the wrought-iron bench in the shade of the wall, and swung his legs, comfortably at a distance from the chatter that spilled down from the windows. Their irregular noise was muted by the smooth tones coming off the crinkled sea beyond the lawn.

He had done his best with Alice Paton, but he realised he was frightened of her. She seemed to make everybody nervous, even when she was not there, and he felt she was spoiling the holiday. It was better being outside, where they would have to call for him if he was needed; he was happier being on the fringes of things, away from the crossfire of those sorts of conversation.

Exactly what had happened the previous day, he did not know. He was not so interested in Alice Paton, who had been absent throughout the evening – what intrigued him was the business with the seal itself. His father had mentioned it, but there remained a tantalising lack of detail. He wondered how Alec had managed it, because it was hard to think of anyone shooting a seal. Some special sort of underwater gun was needed to hit things in the sea; he had seen them in magazines, loaded with a spear and rope.

And what were they going to do with it now it had been shot? He remembered what Miss Mackenzie told him about melting them down into oil, and the men with their trousers crammed with charcoal. Perhaps Alec and his wife would eat some of it and give the rest to their friends.

It might get stuffed, to hang up in a museum. James wanted very much to see the seal before it disappeared completely.

Behind him there came the sound of breathing. Mrs Walker was standing on the gravel path, wearing a powder-blue smock. Her dark hair was held back with a broad red band. She grinned at him.

'Great minds think alike,' she said, holding up her collapsible easel. 'Far from the maddening crowd, that's us.' She slid on to the bench next to him. 'Boring old prep?' Her green eyes were shining, like marbles.

'I love it here. It's heavenly. Don't you think?'

'It's nice and hot,' he ventured.

Venetia Walker arched her throat and a fluty laugh ran out of her mouth. 'Just like your father! You never really say what you think, do you Jamie?' She seemed very pleased, which puzzled him.

'Well, *I* think it's hot anyway,' he continued defiantly. The boy hunched his shoulders in case she should be angry.

'I love you,' she told him, pinching his cheek and delicately shaking it. 'Let's get to work.'

He watched her unfold her apparatus, extending its telescopic legs and screwing them tightly into position. She clamped a thick sketch-pad on to the stand, and began arranging the crimped silver tubes in their box. Most of the paints looked new. The palette that she produced was not wooden; it was composed of many layers of oiled paper which could be torn off and discarded when they were no longer of use. There was a tiny metal cup clipped on to the corner, and she carefully poured turpentine into it from a ribbed green bottle.

'Do you enjoy painting?' she asked.

'Sometimes. We do it at school; in the winter, mostly.'

'Then you must give me your advice. I just can't decide – should I try a landscape first, or start with the sea?'

'The sea,' James said, 'paint that first. It's more difficult.'

She stuck a sable brush in her mouth, sucking its soft hairs. 'You're right. I think it *is*.'

He looked away at the water. 'It's always changing,' he said.

93

Venetia Walker drew a slender stem of charcoal from its brown packet. 'They were right, you know. You really are a clever little boy.' She turned her back on the woven landscape and adjusted the position of the easel, pushing the spikes into the hard soil. She cupped his reluctant chin and scratched a faint moustache on his upper lip with her charcoal. He looked back at her rigidly.

'Thank you, Jamie.' Her neat, polished nail traced the track of the charcoal, and she made a dimple in his cheek. 'Such a clever boy.'

Her eye a gleaming green, like the marbles you see in those plumed heads, in a museum.

. . . . .

'Unit trusts still on the up,' said Cooper shaking his paper into its creases. 'Good good.' His wife held her glass towards him at an angle, to show it was empty. Benson came across with the bottle of hock and offered to refill it.

'I'd keep a weather eye on the old dollar right now, though. Firming up, you know; time to get back in there.' He accepted some more wine. 'In fact it's a racing cert in my opinion. I've written to Tony Straker and told him – sell short, and get back into the market with double. There's going to be a volcano.'

His partner looked thoughtful, both index fingers smoothing his top lip. 'You may well be right,' he said. 'They're not going to sit there in Korea for ever.'

Rosemary Cooper crossed her legs with a hiss. 'Some of us are trying to have a holiday, Richard. Do you mind?'

'There appears to be an apple-core on the croquet lawn,' announced the doctor, who had abandoned his book and was twisting tobacco into his pipe.

'It's a very interesting picture,' murmured Cooper running his finger down the column of figures. 'Take my word for it, on this one: there's a change in the air. And I for one am taking my chances.'

Willis frowned at his fobwatch. 'Don't know about the rest of you, but I'm about ready for luncheon.' He patted his waistcoat and looked wistfully from the window. 'It's gone now, but I could have sworn I smelled flowers in here earlier. Did you catch it. Eh?'

Alice Paton stared stonily at her heap of shells, her hands folded on the green felt.

'But there are none to be seen,' he concluded.

'That's hardly surprising. Even the bell-heather is roasting,' said Rosemary. 'Such a shame.'

He nodded. 'It must have been perfume. Perhaps Kirsty has an admirer.'

'It's never too late, Geoffrey.'

He tugged out his handkerchief. 'Honestly, Rosemary. You are the limit!' He began dabbing at his neck with the polka-dotted prop.

A quarter of a mile out, a grey ship was moving rapidly across the sea.

. . . . .

'I saw something rather unusual,' said Paton adjusting the parallel arrangement of his cutlery. He waved away the sliver of lamb that Benson offered him on the blade of the carving-knife. 'No more for me, thank you very much.' He pressed his lips with the napkin.

'A frigate – I'm relatively certain that's what it was, but she was flying no colours. Not even a marking. I had the 'scope out at the time, trying to see how the devil I could get the dampness out of it. And there she was, cruising across at what must have been, I don't know, twenty knots.'

'Fishing-boat, maybe?' suggested Willis. He scraped red jelly on to his fork. 'Local boys in a trawler?'

'At that speed? I hardly think so.'

The doctor nodded as he chewed. 'Most interesting,' he said, looking quite unconcerned.

'Well, yes, I think it is rather.'

James held the plate out as his father carved, admiring the precise movements as he cut down through the muscle, with that clean thud as the blade slipped through to the bone. 'Take the rest of the claret,' murmured Richard Benson. He lifted the bottle proudly from the sideboard and proceeded clockwise round the room.

'A special patrol, that's what it was,' said Cooper. 'Perfect waters for that sort of thing. Especially on the Sabbath.' The men laughed, but Alice remained silent.

'You would think there was no need for that any more,' she said.

'I know what you mean,' Rosemary nodded, 'but you can never be too sure nowadays.'

'The cold war is a chilly business,' said Cooper.

'You can't put a price on peace,' Paton.

'And there is the threat from within,' said the doctor. 'Couple of chaps in my village I wouldn't turn my back on, I'm telling you. Pinker than your hunting coat, the pair of them. Infil-bloody-trators, never mind their college ties.'

'I don't believe that,' said Alice, staring down at her clenched hands. 'I don't believe any of it.'

Geoffrey Willis looked uneasily around the table. 'Well, maybe you're right, my dear. It's a free world, after all. But it does no harm to be careful. We have the future to consider, after all.'

'Another war,' Paton told her carefully, 'would be a crime. Surely you can understand that? And we need deterrents, like the bomb. Capital punishment on a global scale, if you like. These things are necessary,' he said with every semblance of kindness, 'these things are only designed for your safety.'

'That much is for certain,' agreed Rosemary Cooper, one hand cradling her throat.

.   .   .   .   .

James escaped the croquet tournament without difficulty, since it did not appear they were planning to include him in their teams. He decided he would visit his beach, but before setting off he fastened the new penknife to his belt with a length of string, and slipped it into his pocket. The morning's breeze had disappeared, and the air over the bracken and heather was teeming with columns of midges as he skirted the peninsula.

Two oyster-catchers flittered away from him as he reached the sand, preceding him at a wary distance as he moved along the beach. The sea was a complicated marble of glistening white and blue.

He had a small knapsack over his shoulder, and was planning to collect some driftwood so he could carve something for Mrs Walker with the knife she had given him. There was not much to be gathered as he trod along the shiny band of the high-water mark; most of the bits that looked like wood were the dry, encrusted stems of kelp which split easily and smelled of smoke. He remembered what Alec had said about all wood being precious on the island, as he rooted amongst the weeds and cans and other jetsam.

In the middle of the beach he came across a string of melting jellyfish. There must have been thirty of them, stranded by the last tide, each one no more than a congealed patch with a feathery brown pattern in the middle. James pressed one gingerly with the sole of his sandal. He flipped over the sticky lens with his knife, but it was hard now to think it had ever been alive. The underside looked ragged and diseased.

There was one that was different. Its deliquescent edge had spread out along the sand, but the centre was still domed and blown out, like an egg poaching in a pan. It was much larger than the others, and latticed with purple veins that connected with the translucent filaments coiled around it like a nest. He cut it twice across its glutinous bulb, the strokes at right angles to one another: the slit substance heaved open like a bud, the released tension of the body sending the coloured nerves bulging out through the skin, a bruise leaving the crystal.

97

He collected some fragments of plank and two cork floats, their centres roughly drilled, before reaching the rocks at the right-hand extremity of the strand. It was as far as he had walked in that direction, but he pressed on, away from the sand and over the slippery foreshore blotched with weed.

'Bi glic, Bi glic' went the oyster-catchers, swinging back along the beach.

At the end of the track that led down to the bay beyond he could see the little black Standard parked by the jetty. It was the place where the lobster-boat had docked the previous week, but now there was no vessel tied up there. He could make out the figure of Alec crouched alone on the concrete, along the side of which the half-tyre fenders were strung like leeches.

Alec watched him stumble his way over the dark rocks until he made it to the track and could run down the slope towards him.

'Save your breath, Seumas. One day you'll be needing it.' The carcass of the seal was stretched on the jetty. It was more than seven feet long, and it stank in the heat of the afternoon. James was surprised to see that it was considerably bigger than the man.

With his long flensing knife Alec had already separated the rear half of its skin, revealing the thick yellowish fat beneath. His woollen shirt clung with the sweat of his body, and every few minutes he flicked his hand in aggravation at the blowflies that were weaving around the exposed flesh.

'I saw the Beast,' said the boy, explaining his intrusion. 'I was on the beach looking for wood.' He showed the man his knapsack.

Alec wiped the greasy blade on his rubber boot. The close air smelled of fish. 'Aye, well, this had to be done the day, for the heat. Last night it was that I brought him here behind the *Kilbride*, but I'd no be having the body any place near my house, with the smell on it. The birds have been at him already as it is.' He indicated the bullet-shaped head, its eye-socket torn and bloody. 'Been here all night, so it has,' he repeated, 'and one thing I'm no doing is wasting yon skin.'

'What will you do with it when you've finished?' Now that he had seen the size of the seal, it seemed impossible they were going to eat it.

'I'm thinking it would make a grand wee case for your pencils, man.'

The boy peered at the taut, tubular body and its broad flippers with slender nails on them. They had turned crispy and dry in the sun, like mummified hands.

'But now that you're here, boy, you can help me to turn the big fellow over so I can be finishing the business.' Together, they bundled the seal over like a rug. Underneath, it had been flattened by its weight upon the hard surface and the thick grey hairs were congealed with slime. The soft remaining eye was intact, but James could not imagine what the skeleton within would look like. Clusters of marine parasites squirmed away from the carcass, as it settled.

'Is it an old one?' he asked. The pale underside of the seal showed clearly the place where the man's final bullet had passed through the shoulders.

Alec straightened up and pulled a half-smoked cigarette from behind his ear. 'That he is,' he replied, stabbing a match against the side of its box. 'A fine old bull selchie, and no mistake.' He drew some smoke into his body with a gasp.

'I heard Mr Cooper saying that seals were protected.'

'At certain times of the year, true enough. In the autumn, when the grey seals will be coming ashore for the breeding, that's the time. But that was ages ago they made the law. There's plenty of them now.'

'Was it full of salmon and things?' He still wanted to hear the exact circumstances of the operation, the details of the gun and the way it had been used. The dead seal seemed such a huge thing to have been plucked from the water.

The islander looked bitterly at him through the swarm of his smoke. 'Now, you listen to me, Seumas *ban*, and never be

99

minding the tales they're telling you at that lodge of yours. This selchie is the first I have ever seen killed by a man, since I was a wee boy, and there's no reason for it whatever. The fish are going to survive despite the likes of him, however much he eats, and it's a sorry day indeed when a keeper at Graeval takes his rifle to one of these. My father, now, he would never have agreed to it, but it's out of my hands. That's your grand Willie Grant from Scotland for you.'

The boy looked amazed. 'Why did you do it, then?'

Alec gave a grinding laugh. 'I've a job here, big fellow, and a wife that depends on it. He was wanting me to refuse, so there'd be trouble of sorts. He knows fine well we wouldna' touch a selchie otherwise.'

'But why not?'

'Because there's no luck in it.' He moved carefully around the seal, clockwise, and began slicing once more at the skin. He was beginning to look angry, and James felt he ought to go.

'And what are they saying,' asked Alec, bending to his task, 'that Campbell canna shoot straight any more. Is that it?'

'Nobody's said anything. There's been nothing like that, I promise.'

The man lifted his knife, a gout of blubber on the blade. 'It fair makes me sick,' he said. 'Young Seumas, it has me sick to the bones.'

He could think of nothing else to say. 'I'm sorry, Alec.' He waved goodbye as he disappeared over the rocks, but the islander did not look up, attending to his seal, once more peeling away the rubbery integument of its skin.

When James got back, they were drinking tea on the baked lawn. He sat down once more on the bench and took out his book. Mrs Walker had abandoned her easel, and on the pad there were several sketches of the men in the house-party. On the bench beside him was her palette, splashed and scabbed with paint, like a pale shoulder-blade with a neat hole in it.

X

'Oh dear,' said Rosemary Cooper, looking genuinely fearful, 'I hope I don't manage to break it in some way. It was given to my husband as a wedding present.'

Grant turned the reel over appreciatively, weighing it up in his hand. 'Not a chance, madam. That fellow will stop anything short of a water-horse and no complaining. Money,' he pronounced, 'canna purchase a better wheel than the Perfect. A bonny example of engineering.'

'Honestly, Grant, you're only making me more nervous. Isn't there some old thing I could use instead?'

'Mr Cooper's instructions.' He slipped the reel into its suede pouch and drew the string tight. 'Now that's you ready, excepting the little matter of the flies. There's no sense going without them.'

From the other side of the table Alec observed this performance silently. Since the business with the seal the two men had scarcely spoken to one another and he was cautious of any situation like this where Grant could make a virtue of his superiority.

'I have plenty flies,' he said. Mrs Cooper smiled engagingly at him, narrowing her eyes, but none the less accepted the black japanned tin which the head keeper produced from his pocket.

Grant ignored the other man's interruption. 'There's special tyings you'll find in there that have never seen a shop, and deadly for trout every one. I would think the Blue Pennell would be worth a swim first, if you've any breeze.' He glanced over at Alec. 'But a small size,' he ordered; 'you'll not go too big with this sun.'

'We'll maybe see the look on the water first before deciding.'

'Tight lines, madam,' concluded Grant, 'I must be away for the dogs now or it's me the gentlemen will be shooting.'

The boy's initial reluctance to spend a whole day fishing had dissolved once he discovered that most of the party were going out with the guns. He was interested in learning, but did not want his beginner's ineptitude noticed by his father's friends. On several occasions he had listened to elaborate discussions about fly-fishing, which always made it sound an especially complicated pastime in which you had no proper chance of success unless already an expert. 'Fishing with the fly is the supreme activity of civilised man,' Bobby Paton had told him primly and without explanation. It was the sort of thing schoolmasters said about cricket, and the other games you had to play without any understanding of the rules.

'How terribly exciting this all is,' said Rosemary as they turned off the road and headed up the track towards the lochs. The tyres of the Land Rover left a herring-bone imprint on the peat as they wobbled noisily up the first slope. To their right rose the lunar landscape of Mircavat, where the guns would soon be sounding.

Alec said nothing, but grunted from time to time as the three of them were rolled from side to side on the hard seat.

'And who could wish for a more glorious day?' she went on happily to herself, as the moorland lunged by the window.

'Oh, do look – there's a waterfall. How *pretty!*'

A twirling spout of water sputtered out from between two bulges of yellowing moss, making a viscous trickle; reduced by the weather to a tiny volume, the burn sent out scarcely any noise as it worked its way down through the hardened, corky peat bog. Alec stopped the vehicle and studied the shrunken cataract with professional gloom. 'Hopeless,' he intoned, 'absolutely hopeless.'

They reached the ridge and proceeded at a long diagonal down the slope.

'Loch na Mna,' he said, 'the loch of the woman. Lower than it's been in my entire lifetime.' There was a morose satisfaction in his voice.

In the hollow below them lay an oval expanse of water, its surface chased with a light ripple. At the left end was a squat wooden boathouse with a metal roof, eaten in places by rust. The loch itself was smaller than James had imagined, only a few hundred yards across.

'I wonder who the woman was?' said Rosemary, breathing in deeply as they stood by the oozing rim of the water. 'To have such a place named after you. How mysterious!'

As he struggled with the padlock, Alec looked pleased for the first time that morning. 'It has this name because it's here that the ladies from the lodge generally do their wee bits of fishing,' he told her.

'Oh,' she said in disappointment, 'I thought perhaps somebody lived here, or was drowned. A local woman, that sort of thing.'

The man's voice went hollow as he entered the boathouse. 'Well, Mrs Cooper, that might be. There's mighty few on this island as can swim a single stroke.' He emerged with a slim blue oar over each shoulder. 'Myself's included.'

'You amaze me,' she said. 'With all that sea?'

He shrugged at them. 'Swimmer or no, it would be the same ending out there. The sea,' he confided, 'is sometimes a terrible thing.'

Together they slid the boat down its rollers and towed it through the water towards the car. 'We'll best tackle up right here,' Alec said, 'and have a moment practising in the bay before starting our drift. No sense in hurrying, first day out. And there's a breeze of sorts on the way – we'll have a jabble on the water before very long.'

Now that he had seen the loch, James was suddenly impatient to begin. He felt strangely confident that he might catch something there, even if it was beginner's luck. He watched as Alec assembled his father's old cane rod, screwing the reel on to the handle and feeding the green silk line up through the snake-like rings. A length of moistened catgut was taken from its felt pad and knotted to the end.

'Next thing,' said Alec, groping in his pocket for his own fly-box.

'Are we going to use a Blue Pennell?' asked James, looking into the tobacco-tin of tangled little flies.

The man winked at him slyly. 'We are not.'

Gluck, gluck, went the oars as they pulled away from the shore. The leather bindings squeaked in their rowlocks as the heavy boat swung forwards into the bay. Rosemary Cooper held her trilby on to her head and closed her eyes. 'You know, it's really quite windy once you get out here,' she said.

Alec smiled flatly at her, turning on the thwart. 'I've seen me here in gales that would blow the wave tops off on to yon hill.' He indicated a metal pin behind either rowlock. 'When there's a good breeze running you'd need two men at the oars, just to hold her off the rocks. It's the grandest place in a wave.'

Sitting in the stern, James began to strip line from his reel as he had been shown, pulling it out until the white braided backing began to gape through beneath the remaining coils on the spool. His three flies were now trailing way behind the boat, where the disturbance of its wake was already re-absorbed into the pinches of the ripple.

There was a snatch, followed by a wobbling sensation at the end of the line. 'I've got him, I've got him!' he shouted, turning precariously and giving a heave with his rod. Furiously, he reeled in line from a semi-crouching position, but it came in slackly, the flies skimming the surface as they approached the boat.

Alec watched him patiently, the oars shipped.

'I've lost it.'

'He's no there, right enough; but you never had him in the first place.'

Mrs Cooper bit her lip in sympathy.

'Nothing but a parr,' continued Alec, 'and not worth the catching. He'll have a toothache now, and grow bigger.'

They began a gentle drift down the reedy shore, broadside to the wind. Alec demonstrated the way they should cast; he flicked the team of flies out in front of the boat, and swept them back over his shoulder, the line describing a precise loop in the air before being returned to the water.

'When you hear your line sing like that through the rings,' he told the boy, 'you have made a respectable cast.' He worked the line back through his fingers, tripping the soft-hackled flies through the waves before lifting them off once more. 'Stroke the water with your bob-fly, look, and hang him there a moment before you finish. There's often a fish will follow right into the boat-side, and then he'll take you.'

The first few attempts James made resulted in hieroglyphic tangles of line on the water. Alec said nothing, leaving him to unpick the bird's-nest in the cast with feverish fingers. The line was snagging under the boards in the boat and catching around his shirt buttons and he felt despondent. But later, when he was managing better, he discovered a certain rhythm in the action of flexing the rod, and it became peculiarly satisfying. Once he began to relax a little, he could focus his attention on the body of water before him, without having to concentrate on the tackle. There was a kind of mesmeric effect, like the pendulum of a clock.

Half an hour later, Mrs Cooper let out a shrill cry. 'Goodness, what do I do?' A golden-coloured trout vaulted from the water and struggled to pull line from the reel, but she held it hard and the rod nodded into a curve.

'Let him run, for heaven's sake,' Alec instructed her, manoeuvring the boat into a better position. 'Don't jam the line with your hand.' The fish at last slid over the pear-shaped rim of the landing-net and he hoisted it aboard, dispatching it with three quick blows of his wooden priest. He laid it on the boards of the boat, and the black-tipped ventral fins flickered like the wings of an insect.

'Near enough the pound,' he judged.

She looked warily at it. 'Is it quite dead?'

'Nerves,' replied Alec.

The boy looked sideways at the fish, and then at Mrs Cooper, who had her hands clasped in delight. He felt jealous of her success, and began to worry that he was doing something wrong. He started to cast with renewed vigour, but the more strenuous his efforts to throw the flies a spectacular distance, the less easily the line fell.

As they drifted along under the dark shore where dwarf rowans clung from the miniature cliff, James saw a winking bulge in the water where he had cast beneath the rocky overhang. There was the lightest of tweaks, but that was all. By lunch-time, Rosemary had caught two more fish, but he still had nothing, and his concentration was starting to wander.

'Such bad luck,' she said as they settled for their picnic, 'and you are doing so well – even I can see that.'

He smiled bravely and said it didn't matter, since he knew that was the sporting thing to do. But he no longer believed he was going to catch anything, and felt hopeless at the prospect of the afternoon ahead, flogging the flat water with his line. When Alec returned at two, he found James glumly surveying the loch, picking pieces of heather off their wiry stalks and flicking them into the water.

'It's so comfy,' said Rosemary. 'I feel like a tiny snooze.'

'If you'll be all right here, then, I might take Master James up to the lochan to see if there's a hungry trout or two to be had,' suggested Alec.

'Oh yes, Campbell, do. I shall be blissfully happy here.'

Lochan Uaine lay in a little corrie above the larger loch, hidden from view. It was roundish and spiked all over with rushes, and the water was more sheltered and still.

'What's a water-horse?' asked James as they trudged along the slope, the slender rod like a wand in the man's broad fist. 'Mr Grant said something about it this morning.'

Alec spat on to a rock as he passed. '*Each-uisge*,' he said,
'and likely he's seen plenty in his time. The lochs of Caithness
are surely leaping with them every day of the year.'

'Are they like sea-horses, or what?'

'No, Seumas: it's in the fresh water they were said to live.
Supernatural beasties that came out on to dry land in the
evening and turned themselves into handsome young men
with an eye for the local girls. But you could always tell once
you saw his hair, look, for there would be sand and the odd
trace of weed in it for sure, and that's when the lassie'd take
to her pretty young heels or he'd likely drag her down into
the loch and that would be that.'

'Have you ever seen one?'

'Ach, they dinna exist at all, man. Old wives' tales from
history they are, that would be told at the *ceilidh* by folk with
nothing better to do. Many's the time I've come back home
from a day's work with sand in my hair and heaven knows
what else too – and I'm asking you, do I look like a water-
kelpie?'

He pulled a gruesome face and the boy laughed suddenly.

'Well, this is the pale loch, Lochan Uaine as we have it in
the Gaelic. If you catch no trout here, it's back to England
with you. I'll be leaving you the net, and you can give me the
shout if you need any help. But don't go hooking any water-
horses now.'

The boy watched him disappear over the crest of the corrie,
his halting gait unnoticeable on the rough landscape. As soon
as he was gone, the lochan seemed larger now there was no
other figure to give it scale. He cast fruitlessly from the gently
sloping bank, the trio of heathery flies dragging back towards
him in a long vee across the tobacco-coloured surface of the
water. A small trout flipped its neb out of the water by the
farther shore, sending concentric ripples out under the heavy
afternoon sun. James set off around the bank, carefully skirting
the water's edge as he had been told, to avoid scaring his
quarry. The trout moved again as he came nearer the spot –

he supposed it must be the same one, at any rate it was something to aim for. He pulled the tiny hook of his tail-fly out of the cork handle where it was stuck and plucked some line from the reel.

'Please,' he whispered urgently to himself, like a spell. 'Please. Catch it.' He swished the fly-line on to the water, but in his determination he dropped his arm too far and the cast landed with a long splash. There was a ballooning swirl on the surface where the startled fish had hurtled away to safety, but the boy cast again and again, refusing to admit that it had gone.

For a moment he resented the fact that Alec had left him without any help, but if he could now catch a fish entirely on his own, he realised, the achievement would be greater in the eyes of all the others. He imagined his trout – two of them, maybe – lying proudly on the fish slab under the sprinkler, as the party filed in to dinner, nodding admiringly at the display.

When the noise came it was surprisingly loud, and his head jerked up immediately. It was as if someone had heaved a clod into the centre of the lochan, thick wavelets of water throbbing outwards to the bank. He had not seen the fish but he could see the seismic centre of the disturbance, and plied his line as far as he could towards it. He let it lie for a second, then started to retrieve it carefully between his fingers. The tip dipped, and the line seemed to go solid. James pulled, and nothing gave; the tension set the line thrumming, and then he felt the slow, deep resistance of a fish moving away.

His body was cold and clear with exhilaration, his mind at once concentrated to an intense degree on the surface of the water yet aware of everything that was happening around him. It was not until the fish rolled on the surface and he saw it was a good one that the dreadful possibility of its escape occurred to him, and he began to run along the bank in an attempt to get as close to it as he could. As the trout sounded in the opposite direction, he could feel the taut line cutting through the stems of the reeds in its path. The clatter of the reel's ratchet sounded loud enough to disturb the whole island.

He could not risk leading it half-way around the loch to the place where Alec had left the net, but there was a little slipway of peat close by, where he took up a stance and continued the battle. The trout was not behaving like the ones that had been caught in the morning, which cartwheeled out of the water as they fought to escape: this one was sluggish and stubborn and despite the greater size the boy was succeeding in hauling it gradually in towards him. Barely two yards out in front of him, the fish turned over on the surface, its jaws gaping in a white wedge from the strain he exerted.

Forgetting everything that Alec had told him about playing a fish, he winched at the line and the trout planed in closer. Now its head was out of the water and up on the bank, and the tail flapped convulsively, pushing it further out of its element. James dropped the rod, knelt between his fish and the water, and fell bodily upon it.

There was no loose stone to hand, so he clubbed it on the head as best he could with the butt of his rod; its operculum heaved open, revealing the frail pink slash of gills beneath its cover. Then it lay still.

The fish had a lean body and was altogether darker than the others he had seen. There was a deep bronze sheen to the scales that camouflaged it perfectly against the peat, and it appeared to be twice as long as Mrs Cooper's. Now that it was dead, he felt the tension unwinding in his body and he started to shake. He ran a fingertip along the fish's side and sniffed the peculiar, herb-like smell, and then he stretched out next to it on the moor, gazing exhaustedly at the streaked sky.

Poking a couple of reeds through its mouth and out through one of the gills, he fashioned a temporary sling to carry it until he got back to the net, and it looked quicker to continue on around the loch rather than retrace his footsteps. He walked briskly, paying no attention to the water. The loch had yielded him its prize and he had no further thoughts of fishing. He could hardly wait for the reaction of the others when they saw the result of his victory.

In a dry gully that he had to cross there lay a sheep. It was on its side, but the legs were sticking out instead of being folded. He assumed it was dead. As he stepped down into the dip, he noticed a movement; the animal was raising its head from the splitting peat, but that was all. At first, he made shooing noises to see if it would struggle up and run away, but it merely jerked its head up and down spasmodically.

James approached it with curiosity. The fleece was unusually long and straggly, the wool in places matted into balls. He wondered if perhaps it was a wild sheep: he was not sure if there were such things. There was a purple mark of dye on its neck, so it must have belonged to someone. He crouched a few yards away and it parted its dark yellow teeth as if to bleat, though the low grating it made was more like the sound of fabric bring torn.

There was something else, too, a faint rustling such as a bicycle tyre makes on a damp pavement. It was only when one spilled down on to the dark earth that James saw the whole of the creature's back was a pulsing mass of maggots, their oily off-white colour hardly distinguishable from the wool that surrounded them. The sheep gave another dry rasp, and now he caught the hot vegetable smell of its breath, and he ran to the side of the loch, heaving for air. A sour juice welled at the back of his throat.

When Alec saw the boy waving animatedly to them from the shore he rowed gently over, and grinned at him from a distance. The bows carved up into the sandy beach with a sigh. As James ran along the bank it was obvious he had been excited.

'Hello there,' hailed Rosemary Cooper vaguely. She was tired of sitting in the boat, but was persisting because it seemed such a waste of time to have Alec smoking there and doing nothing.

'Hulloo Seumas – and how many do ye have?'

'I've seen a sheep,' panted the boy. 'It's horrible and dying. You've got to come. It's making a noise.'

She frowned at the man. 'Whatever can he mean, I wonder?'

Alec helped her out of the boat and pulled it further up the sand. He regarded the boy slowly.

'Please,' James implored him, 'come and see the sheep.'

For half an hour they searched but there was no sign of it. The boy could not put it out of his mind and Alec sensed how agitated he had become; he continued scouring the area in an effort to reassure him.

'Well, that's certainly queer,' he admitted as they met back at the gully. 'And you're sure this was the spot?'

'Yes, completely.' His abandoned tackle still lay there next to the fish which he had not even shown to the islander. He felt strangely apologetic about the disappearance of the sheep. 'It must have run away,' he said.

Alec sat down and began tapping a cigarette on his thumb. 'She'd not get far in that condition anyway. Fly-strike it's called. The greenbottle fly: eats the beast alive and poisons the blood. There's nothing we could have done, any rate.' Sinuous smoke streamed from his nostrils.

'It might have gone to find the others. The flock.' He was trying to fend off the man's disbelief.

'That's just it, Seumas. It would be the only beastie for miles: Alasdair MacDonald it is has the grazing hereabouts, and he'd his sheep moved away to yon side of the road back there a fortnight ago. And they were at the fank for the shearing before that, even. This one had the long wool still on her, so you said.'

He began to feel desperate. 'It did, I saw it. And the purple splodge painted on the neck, about here.' He indicated the area above his own collar-bone.

The man simply shook his head. 'I don't know,' he said. 'We've each the separate keel-mark on the island, and there's none but red or blue used since I can remember. She'd maybe strayed down from the north end and been lost a while.' He stood up and clapped his hands decisively. 'The important thing is this trout of yours. Let's be seeing him.'

It no longer seemed such a marvellous fish to him; now that he looked at it, the head was hugely out of proportion to the lank body which had turned almost black. The triumph of its capture had faded with its sheen, and Lochan Uaine, the dark little place that was for some reason called pale, was no longer a place he wished to remember. Disappointment closed heavily around him.

But Alec was whistling in admiration. He held the fish aloft on his thumb. 'That's a beauty, big fellow. Over two pounds, if he's an ounce – and look at the length of him.'

'It's a funny shape,' said James.

'It's the biggest bloody fish out of here for years,' Alec insisted, and dipped it into the water to soften the skin, already crinkled in the sun. The damp hairs clung to his forearm like filaments of weed.

'You're a grand fisher, sir, and no mistake.'

. . . . .

'A cannibal if ever I saw one.'

'You could tie a knot in it. Christ, what a brute.'

The two men glared at the fish under the sprinkler. The boy overheard them as he came through the swing-door with his bucket of ice.

'Aha,' began Cooper, 'home is the hunter. Well done you, that was quite a catch. Give you a good fight, I expect?' He fiddled at his immaculate bow-tie.

'I trust you enjoyed it,' enquired Paton smoothly.

James looked him in the face without smiling. 'Yes, I did.'

'Well, that, of course, is the only thing that matters.'

The dining-room was heavy with the rich fragrance of roasted game. The others had a whole bird each, but James's father had only given him a half, for which he was grateful since the bitter taste of the meat did not appeal to him. There was something similar they used to have at school – it could not have been grouse, of course, but it was called Cook's Pie and was generally served on Mondays. The flesh had the same fibrous texture to it, though it was slightly sweeter. The boys had nicknamed it Mary's Curse after the lumbering school cook.

The fork made a little popping sound as he stuck it into the translucent skin of the breast. Four oily gleets of blood started from the muscle.

'Kirsty has excelled herself once again,' his father informed the party. He brandished his knife at them. 'Say what you like about cheepers, you can't beat a properly-hung two-year-old for taste.'

'How I agree,' said Venetia Walker, her jaws a mask of glistening grease.

'You have to fly them through the oven, no more,' explained Rosemary.

He jabbed at the bisected bird and picked off shreds to be sampled. The square of fried bread on which it was nestling was saturated with intestinal juices that were making the game-chips soggy and pink and causing them to cling to the surface of the plate.

'London,' said Mrs Walker, 'has recently become such a depressing place, particularly at night.' She cocked her head at Michael Cooper and toyed with the silk-covered button on her sleeve. 'We went to the Odeon to see *Roman Holiday* and I can't tell you how dirty it was. Have you seen it, by the way? You must. There was food all over the floor, and paper wrappings. One simply does not expect that sort of thing in Leicester Square.'

He nodded energetically. 'At Winchester, in my day, it was forbidden to eat in the streets, but now it seems to have become some sort of fashion. Italian pizzas, and those American hamburgers. I can't see it myself. Coffee-bars springing up all over the place – good for the commercial market, of course, but, I ask you – what was wrong with good old fish and chips?'

She looked at him seriously, relinquishing her button. 'And the seats. All slashed. Don't ask me why.' She sipped some claret and pressed her purplish mouth with a napkin.

'Cosh-boys,' he said, 'whipper-snappers with no respect for property. Distressingly common, I'm afraid. We had a way of dealing with that in the army, I can tell you. Shave off that hair and stick 'em in a proper uniform – none of those ghastly suits – pitch 'em up against the Mau-Mau for a month or two; see how they enjoy it then. If they're so keen on fighting.'

It was evident from the bleariness of his knowing smile that he was becoming drunk. Venetia murmured her agreement and attended to the wayward button, but the discussion flapped to a broken halt.

'The Great Wen,' added Willis helpfully, chewing on a drum-stick. He masticated his mouthful of meat as if savouring at the same time the significance of what had been said, and then gave a yelp. 'Ouch. Got me.' He scooped his forefinger around his mouth and plonked a crimped fragment of lead on to the plate.

'Must be one of your own, Geoffrey; shot in the leg.'

. . . . .

His father stood in the window twirling a tiny spoon into his coffee.

'I did so enjoy my day,' Rosemary told him. 'I think perhaps I shall take up trout-fishing. It made me feel quite serene.'

'Excellent. And Campbell looked after you all right?'

'Such a sweet man. He can be really quite amusing you know.'

'But not, I hope, impertinent.'

The boy returned with her replenished cup and she put her arm around him. 'But this is the hero of the day,' she said, presenting him to his father.

'Don't I know it?' Benson said, without conviction. 'A tremendous effort.'

James was eager to slip off to bed, but they were soon seated in a rough circle and he could not interrupt the conversation. The men were discussing the politics of the Scottish Nationalist Party and the explosion of the pillar-box in Edinburgh. Only Alice Paton was apart from the group, ensconced at her station of shells.

'Oh no, not just for the moment, Jamie,' Mrs Walker said when finally he found an opportunity to withdraw. 'Not before the game.'

'What game is that?' asked his father.

'Comparisons. I told you. You weren't listening.' She soon had the reluctant party organised and explained her rules. 'It's easy,' she said, 'I'll start. It's a man.'

'If he was an animal, what would he be?' asked Paton.

She released a ringing laugh. 'Oh, a cat. A large tabby cat.'

'Nelson,' suggested Cooper, stretched on his armchair cradling a glass balloon half-filled with brandy.

'Don't be so silly, darling,' said Rosemary, 'just because you don't understand.'

'A type of food?' Benson was rather enjoying the game.

'That's more difficult,' said Venetia, 'but I think: a steak-and-kidney pudding.'

'Alexander the Great,' Cooper said, drawling with alcohol. They went on for several minutes, and then it turned out she was thinking of Geoffrey Willis, but nobody guessed it. The doctor puffed indignantly and rolled his eyes at James. 'Highly unfair,' he protested, 'and all most misleading. A Bentley, that I can just see. Wouldn't mind at all. But really – a cauliflower? A *halibut*? I ask you. Preposterous.'

They played several rounds, and James guessed that Paton had chosen Napoleon, which everyone applauded. He was glowing with enjoyment.

'You'll never get it,' warned his father when it was his turn.

'A flower?' enquired Rosemary.

'Magnolia. Her skin is like magnolia.'

. . . . .

That night, for the first time in months, he dreamed of his mother. She was sitting in a wickerwork chair, leaning over a draped table on which was spread out a huge jigsaw puzzle, none of its pieces fitted together. It was partly the conservatory of their home, and at the same time, as places are in dreams, it was somewhere remoter and unknown.

She did not actually touch any of the fragments with her hand, but was brushing the thick coppery hair back from her temples again and again, scrutinising the surface of the table in dismay. James tried to speak to her, but his mouth was full of a spongy mass that he could not spit out. He became aware of something underneath the table, and then he woke up.

The softness of the night only deepened his feeling of loneliness, and it was a long time before he could settle again into sleep. A low susurrus from the shore seethed through the night, a verminous rustling.

XI

'Well, I'm sorry to be late now, but the sheep were awful bad.' Alec went into the tackle-room where the boy was sitting with a duffel coat folded in his lap. 'They lie like limpets on the road for the warmth in the night, and not even the horn of the Beast can move them.'

He was wearing a heavy-looking coat of ridged, oily material and was carrying a large torch.

'Is it going to be cold?' asked James. Considering the mildness of the late evening air, he thought Alec seemed overdressed for their expedition, with his coat tightly belted, like some detective in a film.

Alec patted his garment. 'You never can tell. We might feel a shower come midnight.' There was something conspiratorial in his look.

When, a few days earlier, he had asked his father's permission he had been expecting an outright refusal, but summoned the necessary courage because Alec had hinted they might see something unusual if they went out watching together.

'What an extraordinary request,' Benson had replied. 'Have you stopped for a moment to consider exactly what might be involved in such a business? Watching for poachers is not some schoolboy game, you know, it's a very serious matter. These local boys,' – he punctured the nose of his cigar with a little spurting sound – 'don't just give themselves up when surprised; it's a criminal activity, and a very vexing one at that. I won't hear of it.' He began rolling the fat tobacco over the flame of his match, the first, yellow smoke burning away from it.

James looked at him apologetically. 'I didn't realise it would be dangerous. I thought it might be fun.'

'Well, that's the point precisely. Campbell should know better: should never have asked you in the first place. But he doesn't think.'

'He said it would be educational: we'd see lots of things. That's what Alec said.'

Benson puffed and turned the cigar to inspect its evenly glowing tip.

'Really? What things, I wonder, apart from local thugs who are no doubt Campbell's friends and neighbours?'

'I don't know: otters, I think, and all the fish in the bay. Apparently it's all different at night. And maybe birds, as well.'

His father took in a mouthful of gin which, combined with the delicious sensation of the first smoke of the day, caused his mood to begin changing at once. Wanting to be left alone with his papers, he waved a hand at his son.

'I will talk to Michael about it; see what he thinks. Now run along.'

The boy had been delighted when, later that evening, his father had agreed. 'I've been considering your little jaunt with Campbell,' he said, mellow with brandy, 'and I can't see the harm in it if you're careful. It seems things have been fairly quiet out there lately – the local boys have got the message. But you must be back here in bed by two, do I make myself plain? I shall have a word with him tomorrow.'

It was not quite dark as they parked the Standard in a passing-place half a mile from the estuary. 'No sense in advertising our presence,' said Alec. The boulders of the scarped hillside gleamed luminously in the pearly light as the dusk slid in along the corries and covered the secret pits and crevices of the landscape. 'Between you and me,' continued Alec, 'I'm no thinking we'll see another living soul. It's Grant that's convinced every man in these islands is after stealing his precious fish, but believe me, Seumas, I'd catch wind of it hours before there was a foot stepped on the moor. But no matter,' he tapped the wing of his nose, 'we'll maybe find a thing or two to keep us busy the while.'

In the dim light, the waves of the estuary looked rubbery against the shore, the coarse sand clotted with disintegrating foam. They settled in a rocky hollow overlooking the river-mouth. Alec pulled out a bottle and there was a clink as it struck against something metallic in his pocket.

'Look,' said James, 'that's the Milky Way. There!'

'Aye; the herring way, the dust of the world. It seems they teach you something at least, in that school of yours.' He considered the sky appreciatively, hot-smelling fumes of whisky dissolving into the evening. 'It's to be a grand night, though something clear.'

The air was practically quiet, but for the occasional squeak of a sea-bird. 'What do we have to do?' James asked him.

'We wait,' replied Alec, squinting through the smoke of his cigarette. 'Until it's properly dark.'

'Have you ever caught a poacher?'

'I have seen people many a time fishing here with nets, if that is what you mean. Poaching – well, that would depend.' Alec sluiced some of the spirit into his mouth and swallowed it with a little grunt. 'It's no so bad watching down here, where ye've the shoreline to listen to, and the fish leaping later. But up in the forest – Christ, man, I've had some terrible nights spent there when I was able to take the hill.' He tapped his leg with his stick.

'Which bit is the forest? I haven't seen that.'

'Sure you have, Seumas; all along the top of Graeval. And once it was covered with trees – the whole island was – cedars, fig-trees, even. That's what it says in the books of history, any ways. And then a wee Norseman came along – Magnus Bareleg his name was – and burned the entire place down. Ach, that was ages ago: in the eleventh century or some such time. I couldn't tell you. The peat burned underground for more than a year after he was away home in the longboat with his princess, or whatever it was he came for.'

'And they never grew again?' He still felt the man might

be making it all up. It was impossible to think of the place in such a way.

'Who was there going to plant them?' Alec replied, the bud of his cigarette growing as he drew on the smoke.

Out in the sea some fish splashed. The haggard coastline was gradually disappearing into the night, and the air was growing chill; he understood now why Alec was wearing his coat, and soon they would need the torch if they were to see anything distinctly. James stood up and shrugged on his duffel.

Alec took another pull of liquid. 'You are the less for that, as the wren said, sipping from the sea,' he told the bottle, the Scotch glimmering down inside him.

'It's very peaceful,' said James. He listened to the noise coming out of the slender throat of the Mircavat River, somehow clearer and higher in the dark.

Alec fiddled with his massive torch and turned it on. 'Too damned peaceful, Seumas, and we should away up river now to patrol. Are you with me?'

In the yellow beam the boy saw that the crest of the rock where they had been hiding was pockmarked in several places with little round pits, in the bottom of each of which lay a pebble. They were like those circular holes in the wall of the school yard, which boys had drilled by grinding a penny around into the soft red brick.

'What are those?' he asked. He imagined some particularly powerful type of shellfish might have eaten away these cavities.

'The cupmarkings, aye. There's one or two of them hereabout, made by the water. The tide and the river make a whirlpool here when they are both high in the winter. It's these stones, look, that they rotate when they get trapped.' He slapped the worn gneiss. 'Takes a year or two to eat into that stuff: that's one of the oldest bitties of Europe you're up against there, fellow.'

James tried the inside of one of the holes with a finger. It was remarkably smooth where the water had whirled the stone around in its socket. He picked it out and held it to the electric beam. The stone was about the size of a songbird egg, and of a translucent, faintly greenish red. 'It's a nice one,' he said.

'Here, now, let me see.' The man's heated breath sounded by his ear. 'The Devil,' he said, 'if you haven't a bloodstone found there. That's a rare piece, boy. You must keep a hold of that, to be sure.'

'Oh. Is it valuable?'

'I'm not pretending there's money it's worth, but there's many a seafaring man carries one in his pocket if he's lucky to find one. Yon's a bloodstone.' The drink was lending him a certain gravity. 'You'll not fear drowning with one of those, and there's a thing to be grateful for.'

The boy studied the thing more carefully. It was unusual, but not beautiful in the way that a marble or a jewel might be. The surface was irregular and grainy, and the colour went a dull grey as he turned it in the light. He slipped it into his corduroy pocket and found an ordinary pebble to plop into the cup in its place.

In the weaving beam they walked up the bank of the river and crossed the road.

'From here it is just under a mile to the lochs,' Alec told him, his breath coming heavily. 'But there's a place maybe half-way up that I'm thinking we ought to visit.'

'Is it a place for poachers?'

The man laughed. 'It just might be, aye.' They pressed on in silence, the torch trained directly in front of their feet. James could no longer make out the river immediately to their left, but the noise of the streamier stretches gradually disappeared behind them, and then Alec switched off the light.

'The tail o'the Long Pool,' he said, pulling the boy down by one shoulder until they were squatting together on the bank. 'Even with this dark, you've to keep off their horizon,' he explained. James was beginning to feel excited: he realised there was a chance of surprising some poachers, and he looked warily around, though without the torch he could see nothing.

'Now, when you've the low water like this,' Alec went on unhurriedly, 'there's maybe three or four fish gets trapped in the pool. They run this far, then the level falls and they're stranded. They canna go backwards at all.'

'What, sea-trout?' He was whispering instinctively. As his eyes recovered from the light he could just see some bulges in the gloom, each one of which might have been the hunched form of a burly man with a net.

'No, man. *Fish*. A salmon is the only one's a fish: but if you name him, he can never be caught at all.'

'Is this the place that they come to net them out?'

There was a pause, while Alec seemed to consider this question, his whisky face hot and close in the dark.

'Well, Seumas, they might. But there's a wee thing I was thinking I could show you whiles we're here, if you'd be keeping the secret after. Just for the fun, mind.' He was sounding cautious. 'What would you say we try a little of the night fishing ourselves?'

The boy was bemused. It seemed impossible that they could do any fishing under such conditions, especially when they were meant to be out watching. 'But we haven't any rods,' he said.

'Now that's just it ,' Alec agreed slowly. 'For we'll no exactly be using a rod. But the blacksmith's fly.' He pressed something cold and steely into the boy's hand; it felt like the head of a miniature rake, ending in some barbed prongs.

'The leister,' breathed Alec. 'The spear.'

'I don't understand.' He had some vague notion that the man was planning to use the weapon against any poachers they might discover at the pool, and he remembered uneasily his father's warning. But Alec's voice was reassuring.

'This is the way of it, then. The leister fits into my staff,

122

here, with the screw. And when the light is put on to the water, if there's a fish there he'll be dazzled. Then we cleek him out, and he's ours. Burning the water, you call it – but it's our secret, mind.'

'But we can't, surely; that's poaching.'

Alec sounded disappointed in his apprentice. 'Aye. But who would know? Aren't we the watchers themselves?'

'Someone might find out; we'd get into terrible trouble.' He conjured the spectres of Grant and his father rising up from the other bank, their accusing faces lit like Halloween pumpkins.

'Ach, what are ye, man or mouse? There's never a risk in it.' His voice softened slightly. 'And would I be after getting you into trouble, d'ye think?' There came the sound of the spear's screw being wound into the shaft of the stick. 'Believe me, man.'

'All right,' agreed the boy. 'Perhaps we could try.'

'Close by the bank is where we need to find him, so I'll have the length of strike. Just you turn on the light when I say.'

The beam of the torch cut through the unbroken glide of the pool, turning a golden brown as it entered the water. The bottom of the river was slimy with the accumulated weed of the summer, but there was no fish caught in the light.

'Quick, man, work it about up here a ways. They must have heard our footsteps – they'll be in the neck.' He scrambled up the bank, hauling himself on the bristly heather.

Where the thin run entered the pool, James's torch discovered three streamlined fish lying very still near the bottom. Creeping below the hypnotising beam, Alec slid his leister gingerly under the surface until it was a foot away from the back of the salmon lying nearest him. The light was shaking in the boy's hand.

'Now,' said Alec, and with one movement he thrust forward and up, like a man shovelling earth, and staggered

123

backwards on to the bank. The skewered fish, small-eyed and dripping, was impaled on all four barbs: they had penetrated the muscle of its back so that it could not even wriggle. Its scales had a reddish, checked appearance, the silver livery of the sea having discoloured through weeks in the warmer fresh water. A kind of wheeze was coming from its throat.

The man clutched the fish's shoulder in exhilaration. 'And now, my fine friend,' he said, bringing a rock down on the thin bone of its skull. Four times he hit it until the dark skin was broken and white. Then he slung the rock into the pool. 'And that portion's for you, Willie Grant,' he said loudly. His movements were quick and efficient as he untied his belt and, twisting the fish carefully off the prongs, hoisted and slid it nose-first into the pocket stitched to the inside of his coat.

'It has the mackintosh lining,' he told the boy. 'We'll maybe need to fix one to your duffel, eh, before very long?' He wiped the leister and unscrewed it rapidly, putting the head back in his pocket. 'And now, who would be any the wiser for the deed?'

By the time they reached the estuary again, James realised he was feeling exhausted. He asked the man what time it was.

'That much I couldna tell you, for I have forgotten my wrist-watch.'

'I wonder if I ought to be getting back. It must be quite late.'

'It'll be no quite time yet, never fear.' The bottle chinked against his teeth.

In the iris-bed nearby, something moved heavily. Alec stiffened and crawled over the sill of rock, clutching the torch, but there was nothing he could see.

'What's out there?' whispered James. He did not share the man's confidence about the likelihood of any poachers.

The man sighed. 'Ocean. And St Kilda, further than you can see. Nothing there nowadays, but a few huts and machines for measuring the wind.' He slithered back towards the boy and extinguished the torch.

James was still more concerned about the noise they had heard.
'There's no one there is there?'
'No, man; they were all shipped away years ago – removed
on a government boat. The place is dead.'
'I mean in the irises there.'
'Not a thing.' He paused to drink. 'You don't know the
half of it, boy, I'm telling you.' Alec had settled down now
and was beginning to get drunk. His mention of St Kilda
produced a rambling sequence of thought. 'These islands are
no place to be for a grown person, not any more, not unless
you're Donald MacIntyre or the likes, who'd a knock on his
head to keep him quiet since the day he was five years old.
Like living in a blasted quarry it is, with the wind mowing
everything flat and the sun won't shine for half of the year. I
know what you think, when the view from yon lodge on a
sunny day is all you see – well, just you pay us a wee visit in
the dead month of February, and see how it is.' He drank
again. 'You don't know the half of it.'
James felt his head go hot with embarrassment. There was
a new aggressive edge to the man's voice, but in the darkness
James could not accurately gauge his mood. He sat apprehensively on his hands and said nothing. He now wanted
very much to go back to the lodge.
'Best time I ever had in my life, since I was maybe a boy of
six or so, was the time I was away from here in the army.
Aye, it was all laid on for you there, even if ye did get shot at
by those Nazzy bastards. And all they could say was "You
must be pining for those misty sheilings, Alec Campbell, with
you so far from home." But, Christ, not me man. You never
saw such places in your life.' He seemed indifferent to the
boy's presence.
'I'm asking you; who'd want to come back here, to
this . . . this *useless* place.'
James felt shocked. 'I thought you loved it here. Isn't it
your home?' A clean smell of fresh fish seeped from the man's
coat as he shifted his position.

'I've a house here right enough, but what else? There's nothing you can bloody well do with five acres of peat – and them sending us chemical fertilizers with no instructions.' He tapped the boy on the arm with his large fist. 'There's not the land, and you know why? It's kept for the deer and their sacred salmon. I seen them in the army, driving around with their pistols and the batons under their arms, oh aye. All right for them, sure enough. Landlords.'

He was drinking sloppily now, and his speech was blurry. James realised he was caught: the man had the torch, and he would never find his way back without it, even if he insisted on leaving. His main fear was not the strange behaviour of Alec but the thought that his father might be waiting up for him.

'By God, things would be different up here if some of us had our way, that's no secret, man, ask Kenneth or the others. I'm telling you,' he repeated, the words swilling around his mouth before he released them. 'You may laugh.' The boy remained tensely quiet.

'It could come to that,' Alec said, contemplating some prospect he had not described.

'I'll have to go,' said James timidly. 'I'm sorry.'

The man ignored him. 'They did it before, Rachel can remember it even. Sent the army up here, and a gunboat on Skye with the sheriffs pulling the babies out o' their cradles and breaking up the furniture when they wouldna' pay their rents. The men from Balallan it was that raided the Pairc, thousands of them; roasted deer all night before the marines arrived. Some of those guns that were hidden in the thatch, they'd not seen the light of day since Culloden.' He started to laugh. 'Christ, aye. The misty sheilings! That's where they'd like us to be. With the sheep.'

James had no idea what he was talking about, but he did not dare inflame Alec any further by interrupting. The man had now fallen to muttering and was occasionally talking to himself in Gaelic.

'Fuck it all,' said Alec and lapsed into a grumbling in‐coherence.

A minute or two passed, and then the boy heard another noise, quite close by, a thumping. Quite suddenly, he felt panic spinning in his abdomen. If there was someone out there, several men perhaps, he would have to face them on his own. 'Please,' he hissed at Alec, shaking him by the foot, 'please, I'm frightened.'

'What's that?' Alec asked drowsily, backing up against the rock, his foot knocking the bottle. He turned heavily and his shoulder caught James on the chin.

'Alec,' he repeated. 'We've got to go. Please wake up.'

'We've got to go,' the man repeated, disoriented by the unwelcome arousal from his stupor.

James turned on the torch and shone it hastily around the estuary. There was nobody there. He kept the light on, as Alec fumbled for his stick, and shook his head as if to clear it: he seemed suddenly to have become docile.

If only the car had been parked nearer, thought the boy; and then it occurred to him that even so he should not let Alec try to drive it. The man was following him with diffi‐culty as they made their way up the slope, the weight of the fish in his coat combined with the effect of his bad leg giving his gait a curious, wounded motion.

'I'm all right, I'm all right,' he kept saying as he swayed.

He made little sound as he fell but there was a protracted moan once he hit the foot of the boulder. James whipped the light round to him and saw him lying with his right leg bent double under his body. His face had gone sallow and he was heaving to catch his breath. Something had happened to his other leg, and he could not move from his position.

'It's useless,' he said faintly, 'you must leave me.'

A musty smell, like celery, reached the boy's nostrils as he tried to lug him upright. The shock of the fall had opened the man's bladder.

'It's useless,' he repeated, obviously in pain.

'Stay here,' blurted James. 'I'll get some help.'

'Leave me. Don't fetch them.'

'I'll run. Don't worry.'

As he fled back to the lodge, the faintest beginnings of dawn were lightening the watersilk of the cirrus sky. He followed the uneven road, swerving to avoid the sleeping sheep. After only five minutes of running there was a sharp pain in his chest, and he had to stop for breath.

He felt sure that Alec must have broken his leg, and that there was someone lurking out there by the estuary, waiting for him. James broke once more into a run, his lungs exploding as he forced himself along the road. He had no idea how long it had taken him, but when he finally wrenched on a light in the hall, the clock read three-fifteen.

James knocked hard on the bedroom door, and a gash of light appeared by his feet. When he turned the handle, the first thing he saw was his father leaning out of the bed, his hand still on the switch of the lamp. And then from the creamy swirl of the sheets there rose the dark head of Venetia Walker, one arm shielding her eyes from the light.

XII

It had been a slow day spent largely in silence, and by the early afternoon he was finding it oppressive. He fidgeted on the window-seat, unable to concentrate on his book, distracted by the enclosed heat that had gathered in the drawing-room from the direct rays of the morning's sun.

He was alone with Alice Paton, who, writing messages on a series of tartan-printed postcards, crouched at her spindly table. She looked up at him occasionally, her eyes narrowed in concentration, and tapped her teeth with the pen.

The flat print swam under his stare; he found he was reading the same lines over again, unable to slide his eyes back across the page with the proper rhythm.

'You're not working,' she told him. 'Why?'

James laid the book down on his knees. 'I'm bored. I want to go out; for a walk.'

'I want,' she repeated, 'I want.'

He looked at her cross little head, bobbing as she spoke. 'Please,' he began, 'may I go out for a walk? It's boiling hot in here. Just along the beach?'

Alice Paton began to shake; she tilted back her head and laughed at the ceiling, making a low sound that seemed to come from her nose. 'Yes,' she said. 'Yes, he'd thank me, your father. He'd thank me for that. Letting you run off.' She waved her pen at him, looking furious. 'What do you take me for?' she asked shrilly. 'Just what kind of person do you take me for?'

The boy gave a shrug. He had given up trying to understand the woman's behaviour. It was perhaps best just to ignore her.

'You're just a child,' she added.

He resumed his book and continued to look at the surface of the paper. He allowed his eyes to dissolve their focus and he began to think of what Alec had told him about gunboats, and babies being hurled out of cots. It was difficult to imagine. Did the gunboats in those days have motors, or only sails? He couldn't quite visualise the soldiers either, with their red coats and those tall hats, marching across the heather. In pictures you always saw them in a desert, or fighting the Russians amongst a lot of cannons. He was afraid Alec had been making most of it up.

People did make things up, all the time, he understood that now. But sometimes it was too confusing. He thought back to the day when his mother had rung home saying she must speak with Mrs Cassell. She was in a department store, she had told him, and she had had a little fall. His mother repeated her wish to speak to Mrs Cassell, but she sounded strangely muffled and distant.

It wasn't until his father returned home early from the office – earlier than he had ever done – that James realised something was wrong, and decided to leave the house. He spent that afternoon roaming the garden on his own.

'You mother gets ill,' his father had told him. 'She takes medicines that sometimes don't agree with her. She's decided to go and see a doctor until she's better again.'

She'd been arrested in a shop. He'd only discovered that later by standing in the garden and listening to a conversation that came clearly through the mullioned windows of the sitting-room. James had never been exactly sure who was in the room on that occasion, but he remembered distinctly the choked voice of the housekeeper saying, 'Oh, sir that can't be right,' and then the calmer tones of Mrs Walker telling his father that in all conscience it was better this way, before something really serious took place.

He didn't realise Alice was there until she struck him lightly on the chest.

'You think I don't know, but I'm not such a fool.' She was

stooping slightly over him. The boy looked amazed. She laid the back of her hand against his bare arm and pressed it. The fingers were cold and felt knobbly. 'You're a child. But I understand, I know what they're up to, the others.' She nodded at him, as if in reassurance.

Clutching his book to his chest, James shrank back instinctively along the seat. His head heaved and his tongue was like meat. 'I'm sorry,' he mumbled, 'I don't know what you're talking about.' He could see the confusion in her face, now bent over his, but he knew he needed to get away.

'Go on then. Disappear again, if you want to. I couldn't care. It's got nothing to do with me.' Alice Paton shook his shoulder quite roughly.

He scrambled up, and hurried for the door. The important thing was just to get outside. 'I couldn't care less,' she shouted after him, as he clattered down the stairs. He made it to the courtyard, his heels making dull detonations on the cobblestones, his thighs aching already, after the long run of the previous night.

Birds yelled above him as he panted along the shore, drawing in the salt and the warmth of the breeze. Soon, he thought, they would be going home again, and then he would be back at school away from all the strangeness of these people. He paused briefly to catch his breath, before clambering up the terraces of the headland, its laminated surface spread with the dark viscera of weed.

His father's anger did not worry him any more, he felt quite distant from such things. There was only the glistening rock under his hands, the sand between his fingers, and the light coming at him along the sea. He would explain to Alec, and everything would be clearer.

The small house steamed in the distance like a trawler.

.   .   .   .   .

It was the first time his father had even entered the bedroom. 'I'm not having you late for breakfast, on top of everything

131

else. Get yourself dressed.' He had nudged the boy with his elbow. 'I want some words with you.'

James took some time to emerge properly from his exhausted sleep. He saw his father standing by the window, staring stiffly out of it, his hands clasped behind him in an unaccustomed pose. There were images dissolving and then lurching up again, of bright lights glaring through a body of water, boulders moving up a hill.

'What's happened?' he asked, levering himself from the mattress with one arm. There was a sweet, flowery smell in the room, but it was not the same as his father's usual cologne.

'What happened last night was disgraceful. I am greatly displeased. I was just beginning to think you were old enough – grown-up enough – to be trusted, but it seems I was mistaken. You gave me your word.' His voice had the precise tone of a prepared speech. 'Get dressed. You broke your promise, and there was nearly a very serious accident.'

Richard Benson would not look directly at his son.

'Are you listening to me?' said the man, his head inclined towards the bed.

'Yes, father. I'm sorry.'

'I should think you bloody well are.'

James threaded his elastic belt, and hooked its metal snake into the eye of the buckle. He concentrated mechanically on the business of dressing himself.

'It won't happen again,' his father went on, 'it won't happen again because from now on, you are going to stay here in the lodge, unless I say otherwise. Do I make myself clear? Do I?'

'Yes.' He wanted to ask how Alec was, but he didn't dare. His memory of the night was reassembling itself, certain events in particular.

'Very well.' His father cleared his throat, twice. 'There's one other thing, before we go down. Last night, Mrs Walker was very upset. She is, as you know, an old friend of the family, and she's most unhappy.' His voice had risen just perceptibly. 'My friendship with her is an entirely private matter, and I don't expect you to understand. But we will not mention it again, to anybody. It is nothing that need concern you.' He handed the boy a hairbrush.

James nodded. His father looked different that morning, but he was not sure exactly how. His eyes seemed to be smaller.

'And do tuck your shirt in. You look a mess.'

. . . . .

He walked quickly through the garden, with its seared and salt-burned vegetation. Christina was in her kitchen cleaning the stove, and she did not appear surprised to see him.

'Ah, Seumas, what a day,' she said, raising both palms at him and flapping them once, in greeting. 'You'll take tea,' she told him, gathering the boy down into a chair, 'for himself is still asleep there, and no wonder. No wonder.'

'Is Alec all right?'

The woman stood with her back to him, and wiped her hands repeatedly on her apron. 'He'll be fine once he's mended,' she replied, trying to sound dismissive. As she spoke, she drew in a long draught of air, like someone about to dive.

'I just wanted to say sorry. For not doing what he said.'

Christina Campbell appeared not to heed his apology. 'There's only the evaporated today I'm afraid, for the fresh curdled with the heat on the road down. Will that be suiting you now?' She tipped some viscous yellow milk on to the rotating surface of his tea. 'And here's sugar, should you wish it.' She sat down opposite him. 'That doctor was very kind. Strapped him up, and no charge. But I'm thinking he'll lose his employment when the word reaches Mister Kershaw. It's to be expected.'

'Gosh, I do hope not,' said James. 'It's my fault, really. I was worried he was badly hurt.'

She patted his hand. 'It's grateful I am to you, Seumas, for doing as you did. You were the grown man of the two, and

133

there's no fault in it. Besides, that shore's never a place to be lying alone all night, and surely he could not have moved.' She looked at him thoughtfully.

'There's to be changes in this house once he's back on his feet, I'm telling you.'

'You see, we didn't have a watch.' The boy could not tell if she was blaming him.

'Well, I'll be rousing him once you've had your cup. But he's not that happy in his mind just now.' Her hands kneaded the apron again. 'It's not only the drink he's taken. You'll maybe see for yourself. He'd be wishing to speak to you, of that I'm sure.'

James thought he could see tears starting from the corners of her eyes. 'I can't really stay very long,' he said. 'I'm meant to be working, in the lodge.'

She blinked at him. 'He'll miss your company, that he will. Like you were a son of his own.'

· · · · ·

Dr Willis had assumed the role of spokesman for the events of the previous night, and he recounted the details with the relish of one whose life revolves around miniature dramas.

'Virtually insensible from drink, I'm afraid to say. And a damned heavy fellow, to boot – a dead weight to carry up to the car. Eh, Richard?' He forked kedgeree towards his mouth, waggling a forefinger to indicate he had not yet finished his story. 'Smelling none too sweet, either. Stank like a fish – hadn't noticed that before. Of course people like these believe in preserving the bodily oils,' he went on, 'and their concept of hygiene is altogether different.' He chewed on his mouthful with a beam of satisfaction.

Rosemary Cooper put her knife and fork together daintily. 'How very unpleasant for you, Geoffrey. Was he in a very bad way?' She looked genuinely concerned.

'Oh, seen worse my dear. You know. Nothing actually broken, happy to say. But he'll be a touch green around the gills this morning, and flat on his back for a day or two, that's for certain. Nothing to take his weight, do you see?'

'It will give him ample time to consider the precariousness of his future,' observed Paton carefully, 'for I would imagine there will shortly be a vacancy for the position of under-keeper here.'

Benson nodded. 'He'll be no great loss to the estate, in my opinion. I shall indicate as much in my letter.'

'What will he do, poor man?' wondered Rosemary Cooper, crunching at her toast.

'Same as the rest of them,' Paton said, 'crofting, odd jobs. He'll survive. They all do.'

The boy transferred the bank of rice from one side of his plate to the other, using his knife like a snow-plough. Several grains spilled over on to the table, where they lay like hard little grubs. Quickly, he pushed away his plate.

'But who will handle the dogs, I wonder?' enquired Willis.

Although he heard what they were saying, James did not feel as if they were discussing anyone he knew. Their remarks had nothing to do with the man he had last seen out in the night, lying on the hill like an insect that had collided with something. He was glad they were not involving him directly in the conversation.

His father shook his head. 'All taken care of, Geoffrey. Grant's rustled up some chap from the village. And Venetia's going to lend a hand too. Aren't you?' he said, looking at her intently.

She smiled and said nothing. She had scarcely spoken throughout the meal.

'Talking of which,' Benson continued, looking with a certain deliberation at his wrist-watch, 'we should be thinking about making a move. We're on the high ground this morning, for our sins.'

There had been no reference to his own part in the incident, but once the men had gone Alice Paton turned to him and said, 'I expect you were rather frightened out there, with that man.' It did not sound like commiseration, neither was it reproachful.

'Yes,' he replied. 'It was dark. And there were some noises.'

.   .   .   .   .

His few movements, as he lay on the bed, were stiff and precise, like those of a much older man.

'Just look at you,' said his wife, her tongue tutting as she fussed with the pillows. 'And still not shaved yet.' On a stool by the bed was a tin bowl, with soap and a cut-throat razor.

Alec strained to clear his throat, a laboured sound like a gear changing without the clutch. He looked at the boy as if at a stranger, his eyes latticed with bloodshot vessels.

'Hello, Alec,' said James. There was no chair, so he stood by the door, the man regarding him vaguely.

'I'll be fetching fresh water for that face,' said Christina, clearing the stool. 'Sit you down now.'

The man's slowness made James suddenly uneasy. He had intended to be cheerful, but he now wondered whether something more serious had happened to Alec, whose face looked as dull as earth. He sat on the low stool, and stared at the bedclothes. 'I'm sorry. Your leg must be jolly sore.'

There was a pause. 'No,' replied Alec flatly, 'it's better.'

'I just came to see . . . I can only stay a second. I'm not really meant to be here.'

'Aye,' said the man. 'Has she given you tea?'

'Oh yes. Thank you.' James plaited his fingers. He was sorry now he had decided to come to this hot little room with its smell of sweat.

Alec coughed. He jerked a thumb towards the door. 'She'll no let me have the cigarettes.'

'I thought you'd broken your leg. It happened to a boy at school, playing rugger. I saw it.' At least he had delivered his explanation.

Alec appeared not to register what he meant. He closed his

eyes and passed a large hand across his face, brushing his stubble. It sounded like toast being scraped.

'There was something there, boy. If they hadna come . . . I'm not saying. But I should be thanking you. Something there, breathing like the bull.' He was clearly quite exhausted, and there was still whisky in his breath.

'Maybe it was a bull. I heard something. I told you.'

Alec shook his head, to indicate that he could not remember. 'There's only the one bull for this island, and that's away to the south just now. It was not the bull. No.'

'I'm glad you're safe.'

'Maybe so. It was a terrible night.'

The boy stood up. 'Yes, I'm sorry.'

'Christ, man, but I could kill for a smoke.'

. . . . .

'I'm afraid I'm not quite with you,' said Rosemary Cooper. 'I thought Richard's instructions to us were altogether clear.'

Alice just laughed at her. 'He's not our child. He said he wanted to go out,' she shrugged. 'I'm not a governess.'

'Well, yes, but Richard is rightly very concerned about the boy, and frankly I can't imagine what he will say if he returns to find we have let him out of our sight. Really, Alice. At times you surprise me.'

'I'm not his mother.'

Rosemary Cooper stood by the fireplace and balanced a delicate foot on the fender. 'He has no mother. To speak of. It is up to us, that's what we are here for. After all, we could hardly expect Venetia to look after him. Not under the circumstances.'

'Forgive me. I thought we were having a holiday.'

'Where did he go? I think I should follow him.'

'I don't know, Rosemary. He went for a walk on the beach.' She shuffled her postcards into a precise stack.

Rosemary smiled sweetly at her friend. 'Was this entirely wise I wonder?'

137

'I hate this place,' Alice Paton told her firmly from the lonely table.

.   .   .   .   .

'Jesus, the fish.' Alec made a convulsive movement as if to sit up. 'He'll find it.'

'Who will?'

'That Grant. He'll be away snooping, once he's off the hill and the guns cleaned. Sure as rain.' He was suddenly agitated.

'Where was it? The fish?'

'You've to find it, man. I canna mind now. But it's no in my coat, so there's something I must have done with it.' He looked at James unsteadily.

'What shall I do? Bring it back here?'

'Ach, no. He'll be round here later, too, sniffing for scales. Christ, it's happened before. Have me before the sheriff, if he could. Bastard.'

'But I haven't got time. I'm late.' He felt trapped, uncertain what to do.

This new problem had focused Alec's mind. 'If our fish is found, with the cleek marks upon him, then I'm sunk.'

'Couldn't Mrs Campbell . . .?'

'And whatever reason would she give, to be hunting around on that land? No, Seumas, we'd that fish taken together, and he must be found. Take him to my Auntie Rachel's. She'll be knowing what to do with a grilse.'

James stood, looking doubtful. 'I can't.'

'Listen, Seumas *ban*, we burned the water of Graeval together. You're an island boy now.' Alec was not smiling. 'There's a thing to be done.'

In the daylight it was quite simple to retrace the path they had taken in the dark. He found the spot where Alec had fallen, and, a few yards to the left, lay the stiffened fish where he had flung it for safety.

He could hear the popping of the guns away up on the dinosaur peaks behind the lodge, and realised he could get back before the men returned for tea as long as he went there at once. He would throw the fish into the sea, where the keeper would never find it, and tell Alec it had disappeared. If he did that now there would be no more trouble.

James picked the salmon up by the hard wrist of its tail and lugged it towards the shore. He felt sure he was doing the right thing, but as he walked there came quite suddenly into his mind a picture, strangely vivid, of himself standing by the large table in Miss Mackenzie's room, the fish lying on a plate between them. The scene had the clarity of something remembered rather than imagined, so that he stopped for an instant, surprised at the sensation.

'That's lovely,' he thought he remembered her saying, 'a gift from the sea.' She was drawing her hand along the length of the salmon, in appreciation. 'Lovely.'

Then it was over, and his mind was entirely made up. There was a sense of release, an overwhelming feeling like the experience of the bell ringing at the end of a class, when the anxiety of being questioned dissolves in a second, and the recent past shrinks to nothing. He began to run.

In the light of that early evening the birds were silhouetted, drifting like cinders against the sun.

XIII

The thin breeze feathering the bay was so gentle it hardly disturbed the air, nor the web of gunmetal smoke suspended above the roof of her low house. Urgency and the dead weight of the fish were making him pant as he clambered through the close heat of the evening, around the inlet where the sea had taken a bite out of the coastline.

'*Thig a 's Tigh*', she said to him in welcome. James laid the fish down on the clean doorstep and entered, for the first time without knocking. The room was bitter with blue peat-smoke, and the closed window allowed no current of air.

'I'm glad that you've come,' Miss Mackenzie told him, seated at her table with a woollen shawl hugged around her shoulders. There were mail-order catalogues scattered in front of her, their covers ringed with the marks of cups. She did not get up, but watched the boy stand, one hand leaning against the table, heaving for air.

'I'm sorry,' he gasped, 'sorry to be in such a hurry.' James collected himself, unsure of how to explain his sudden arrival. The acrid thickness of the air made him cough as he hauled it into his lungs, and it was strong enough to make him feel dizzy.

Miss Mackenzie snuffed the air several times. He thought she must be smelling the scaly slime that was drying on his hands and had left a congealed shine down the right leg of his trousers. Head still bent over the table, he stretched out a palm to her: 'It's the fish,' he explained, apologising.

'No, no, there is something else.'

He was amazed she could smell anything through the smoke.

'Flowers,' said the woman, shaking her head. James recovered his breath, and looked up at her; she was frowning. 'I have the water here for you ready,' she went on pouring some from a jug, and stirring a spoonful of oats into the cup. 'This will take the heat off you, Seumas, though here in the island there's seldom a need to be running.'

He gulped the drink quickly, savouring its delicate flavour of earth. 'I'm late,' he explained, 'that's why.' James looked at her over the glazed rim; how could she have known he was coming?

'Yes indeed. I was hearing it all from John Angus the Post, but an hour ago. That nephew of mine – imagine him using a fine boy like you to run his errands, with him having caused the only trouble himself.' She clucked her tongue and peered at him as he settled. 'This heat,' she said, 'it's not right.'

'It's boiling,' agreed James. He couldn't think why she was so wrapped up if she was uncomfortable.

'Well, I'm that old I don't feel it. But I do know it's not right; and there's the need for a change. The worst of it is, there's hardly a wind. Not for a month now. That was never a thing I knew before, in my life.'

She was quiet for a moment, considering this as she peered into the grate. The boy chewed on the sour oatflakes in his mouthful of liquid. The room seemed to go very still. 'I mind when I was a girl,' she continued, her voice slow and dry, 'there was a summer when a storm shook this island for weeks at a length. It was that loud you could not sleep at night for the calling of it, even in the black house yonder, where the walls are so thick you could scarce catch a noise otherwise. I was around at *Cnoc Mor* – the great hill as we know it, though it's none but a small mound – behind the dunes there, and I had my sister Maureen by the hand, a little girl as she then was, when a blow of wind lifted her up into the air and me the only thing holding her down. She turned around twice, like a windmill, before I could pull her down.' Her eyes described two circles in the direction of the blackened ceiling as she recalled it.

'It sounds terribly dangerous,' said James.

'That would depend: as with all things, there is the good and the bad. Certain of the winds brought us weed from the sea, for the lazy-beds, and the bright harvest of fish. Others brought sorrow; the grey wind from the mouth of the west, now, that's one we would be often fearing, and the white wind that proceeds from the south, and sets a crest on the waves. But never a summer like this with them all absent.'

It was hard for him to imagine the place under such conditions; the grip of the heat wave had been so persistent, the idea of a wild and frightening island didn't seem possible, though he knew from what everyone had said that it was normal and true. One winter, Alec had assured him, the gale rolled some boulders over a cliff.

'I suppose it must get very cold later on,' he said.

'Aye. Soon enough, soon enough – white feet, white wings, white hands.'

The boy thought for a minute; cold hands were usually red, or blue, the picture of them turning white was disturbing. He could see the frozen birds though, locked into the ground, their wings shining and hard, the shoes of the islanders white and gleaming as they gathered them for food.

'They used to say that *Gaoth Tuath*, the North Wind, the black one, had three sons,' said Miss Mackenzie, 'and those were the names on them. Beautiful they were, but so bright that one would die at seeing them, so they went away from the sight of men and became invisible, and now it's only traces of each that you can see – the white waves made by his feet, the white plumes of the snow he brings, and the icy hand that stills the waters and the grasses.'

James listened to her admiringly. 'You do know some strange stories,' he said, 'I've never heard that before.'

'*Se am fear as fhaide beo as mottha chi* –the one who stays alive the longest sees the most. But it's the poor manners I have, Seumas, for unless I'm reading your face wrong, you've to be away, and me seated here enjoying your company, and telling the tales.'

'Well, yes, I'm afraid I have to be off. But I brought you the fish.'

She stood stiffly up. 'Yes, yes. We've never to be leaving it there in the sun for folk to see it and start their talking. Fetch it here now, and we'll set it straight over the fire, when I've the water boiled.'

Together they laid the salmon on the blue plate. She passed her right hand along its length, as if appraising it. 'I'm thinking this creature may cost my nephew dearly when his night's work comes to be reckoned,' she said, 'but now it's here, we should be grateful and make a meal on it.'

'He hurt his leg quite badly, but I think he's getting better.'

'It's not the first time,' said the woman wearily. 'He was for ever that head-strong, even as a boy, and now there's the drink. *Is dona an leisgeul a'mhisg* – but drunkenness is no excuse.' She reached up for a large metal container on the shelf above her sink.

James protested automatically. 'But it wasn't his fault. Really. It was bad luck, an accident. We didn't have a watch, and it got dark.' He realised as she turned that his loyalty was not necessary.

'Sure, and I know Alec Campbell, and the ways of him. Especially since that last war, which could have been the making of him, if he was to survive it. He's a good man, Seumas *ban*, that you can tell; but there's an unhappiness that's on him now, and I'm thinking it will never leave him.' She lugged the fish-kettle over to the fire and hung it on the hook above the grate. 'The beginnings of sorrow are small, but we've to watch for them, like the gigelorum that lays its egg in the mite's ear.'

James could see that she was concerned. 'I'm sure he won't lose his job, or anything,' he said trying to sound reassuring. 'I think it has all blown over.'

She began to pour water into the kettle. 'There would be

nothing for him here if he had not that employment. There's not a living to be had from the croft, and he would have to move away, like the others. A shame it is Christina never had a child, for they've no family.'

'There's you.'

'I'm just an old woman. There's no person should waste his time thinking on me.' She said it without any trace of self-pity. 'Though, if you've a mind to help, you could surely fill this vessel for me whilst I attend to my fire, for there's hardly a red flame in it for the boiling.'

She stooped to rake the rusty ash away from the half-consumed peats. A billow of dark smoke came out of the grate and, as she stretched across to replace the poker, the boy saw a glowing fragment slide on to her sleeve.

'Miss Mackenzie!' he shouted, 'be careful – your arm.'

Straightening with a jerk, she grasped her sleeve and examined it. There was no sign of a burn on the rough, oiled wool. She looked at him curiously, and held out her elbow towards him.

'I was sure a bit of peat fell out. I'm sorry.'

'May be you imagined it, for there's no harm done.'

He scanned the hearth, looking puzzled. 'It gave me a fright. I thought it would burn you.' There was nothing on the stone except soft looking feathers of ash.

'*Rudhadh an teine* – surely it was nothing but the bloom of the fire. Bride be blessed for it. You should not be concerned. The fire in the hearth is a friend in the house, there's no evil in it. Seventy years and more I've been smooring it each night before sleep – *smaladh an teine*, as my mother taught, and thus do the dead bury the living. No harm from the hearth.'

James thought she was shivering even more than usual; he was worried he had frightened her with his sudden shout.

'I thank you for your fish,' she said politely, 'which you helped the fool Alec to catch, in this time of drought. That was a skilful thing. Will you come again to visit the *cailleach*?' Miss Mackenzie smiled gently at him.

144

'Oh, yes, I will. If I can.' He raised his hand to her, and made for the door. 'Goodbye.'

'What's my name, Seumas?' she asked him.

'Miss . . . Rachel,' he corrected himself, 'Rachel.'

. . . . .

The long skin of the sea was ripening under the sinking sun as he dashed back along the shore. A pair of oyster-catchers, huddled on their red legs, shook themselves as he approached and began mincing reluctantly away across the wet sand.

He had not realised how long he had spent in her house, but now when he looked at his watch it was already half-past six and with a sudden urgency the need to be back at the lodge entered him like a flurry. The requirements of the Graeval routine caught him up once again, but his previous fear for punctuality had faded, and in its place was a sense of something different, a feeling that this was not the only thing that was important after all. His sandals were saturated and squelching with sand, but he whooped out aloud as he ran and the faint, sucking noise of the surf mingled with the quick rhythms of his breath.

Taking the stairs two at a time, he reached the door of the drawing-room and paused to look in. There was no one there, but the sound of bathwater that thundered down from the corridors above reassured him he still had time to get ready for dinner and maybe escape being discovered. He was about to bolt up to his room when he heard the clacking noise of somebody coming across the stone-flagged hall beneath him. Instinctively he popped his head over the banisters, and saw Mrs Walker standing there, holding an arrangement of dried flowers.

She looked up at him. She had already changed, and was wearing a dress of thin blue silk, and black suede shoes. James's eyes stared at her, but she said nothing, and moved away towards the dining-room where the echo of her sharp heels was swallowed by the thickness of carpet.

It was Rosemary Cooper, in her fragrant shawl, who repri-
manded him quietly. She waited until they were descend-
ing for their meal and then, drawing one arm around him,
murmured: 'It's not really fair of you, darling, to play truant
like this. Not fair on Mrs Paton, on any of us. I do understand, but it puts us in a terrible pickle – I mean, I had to
tell your papa the most ghastly fib, or he'd have been furious,
livid with us all.'

'Yes,' admitted James, genuinely sorry to have caused her
embarrassment. 'But I did want to go out. It was hot.'

'I'm sure. Anyway, I told Richard you had gone up to rest.
But, please, never again. You see, it simply isn't *fair*.' She
brushed his ear with the tips of her fingers.

He felt unusually tired when dinner was over, and was con-
tent to take no part in the conversations. Something was making
him feel slightly uneasy: he could not tell what, and it was not
exactly unpleasant, more like that distracting sense of anticipation that he felt before having to play in a match at school. He
was finding it difficult to concentrate on what was happening.

'Are you leaving us so early?' enquired Alice Paton, raising
both hands at his quiet announcement. 'I should have thought
you'd be full of beans,' she added, 'after that long rest of
yours this afternoon.' He stared at her uncomfortably.

'Well, I think I will go up, if you don't mind. And read.'

Rosemary Cooper pressed her sampler into her lap. 'Why
don't *I* come along and read to you?' she cried. 'I should love to.
It's ages since I did, and I'm fed *up* with this needlework. May I?'

He bit his lip, embarrassed at the suggestion and unable to
think of a way out.

'In about ten minutes or so – when you're comfy?' She
looked so imploring that he smiled his assent.

'How clever you are,' said Alice tartly, 'with your sugges-
tions. I should never have thought of that.'

Rosemary Cooper made a friendly smile. 'Ah, well, Alice,'
she said, 'I have a son of my own. Remember?'

· · · · ·

He would have preferred to be left on his own, but at least he was away from most of them; the men with their backs turned, huddled over their cards and their glasses, and Mrs Walker, who did not speak to him, and Mrs Paton with her face pale as concrete. There was never any danger of them venturing up to his quiet room, and he was grateful at least for that. There was something comfortable about being able to retreat there, high up in the otherwise noisy lodge.

As he took off his shirt he noticed a brownish mark on his forearm, the right one; it looked like an old bruise. He pressed it gently, wondering where it could have come from. It felt slightly inflamed, but was not especially tender. James shrugged on his pyjamas and clambered between the sheets, crisp, abrasive, yet welcoming.

He paid little attention to her reading, but Rosemary Cooper seemed to be enjoying herself, perched at the foot of his bed. She read intently, and did not look away from the page once, her voice assuming a breathless tone that was unlike her usual way of speaking and was soporific in a way that made the story itself sink beneath the sound of the words themselves.

' "It is winter," answered the Swallow, "and the chill snow will soon be here. In Egypt the sun is warm on the green palm-trees, and the crocodiles lie in the mud and look lazily about them." '

But James was thinking instead about the children of the wind, trying hard to imagine what each might actually look like. It was confusing when you remembered their different colours – how could there be a black wind? And what would happen if they all converged together? It seemed a very confusing way to explain the weather and the transparent air, yet the old woman had told him the story as if it were common knowledge, and now she had done so he found it difficult to think of the wind except as a person, or a lot of different people.

There was something about Rachel Mackenzie as well;

again, he could not quite put his finger on it, especially now he was growing sleepy, but she had seemed a little frailer, more vulnerable than before. He imagined what might come to pass if Alec had to move elsewhere, and she were to be left on her own. James decided he would go and visit her again, as soon as he could get away without too much difficulty. Maybe he would find something to take her as a present.

'"Leaf after leaf of the fine gold the Swallow picked off, till the Happy Prince looked quite dull and grey,"' she intoned, her eyes wide with delight.

It was clear to him now, whatever else was going on, that he need only appear on time for things at the lodge, and he would be left to his own devices. He had to be polite, of course, and be tidy, but even his father had not tried to interrogate him about how he had spent his day, and James was a little surprised he did not feel at all guilty at having disobeyed him. Besides, he had helped Alec out and kept his word there, and a strong sensation of satisfaction about that began to close in on him, and make him feel secure enough for sleep.

He closed his eyes.

'"Then the snow came,"' she read, '"and after the snow came the frost. The streets looked as if they were made of silver."'

The black wind was encircling a peak, his limbs rolling, his fingers hammering over the crags and the scree. There was a strange, metallic echo of stone being struck. He could see the face of this wind, a mask of furrowed smoke, cheeks puffed like the illustrations in the corner of an old map, but it was not frightening.

Three white creatures came pounding towards the mountain, but they were indistinct, caught only in snatches. One seemed to be kicking snow, and another to be hurling hail, but their faces would not come into focus, and the air was a whirl of weather and light. A figure with an halation of frozen hair loomed briefly and then dissolved. Seabirds blared in the distance.

Rosemary Cooper finished the story in a whisper: ' "And in my city of gold the Happy Prince shall praise me" ', she read, seeing the boy had fallen asleep. She kissed him above the eyes, and left the room carefully. It had been a lovely evening.

A small boat, pitching heavily towards the shore, seemed to have sails of pale bark. On the deck, there was somebody hauling in a rope, back turned, streaming, and then he was standing there next to him, grasping the twisted hemp, and heaving it in.

The figure disappeared, the line came in, and there was nothing on the end.

'Poor dear,' said Rosemary Cooper to her husband, 'he's quite dead to the world.'

'What's that?' asked Michael, his head full of bridge calculations.

'James,' she said. 'He looks so sweet, just lying there asleep.'

He nodded. 'Ah, yes, of course. Lucky chap – kind of you.'

The dream deepened and became more clear. The sky rained down feathers of snow, and along the deck and the prow there lay the white wings of birds, frozen to the deck, but he was not aware of being cold. There came the sound, which he only now recognised, of someone rowing him slowly away from the shore.

XIV

Alice looked up and frowned, as if a small distant noise had attracted her attention. 'Finished what?' she demanded. Rosemary Cooper was walking around the room and holding the completed embroidery in front of her at arm's length, turning it this way and that, like someone admiring some new bracelet.

'It's gorgeous,' Venetia told her with a deliberate gasp. 'I don't know – honestly, I would never have the *patience!*'

'It's going to be a cushion,' said Rosemary, nodding appreciatively. 'I have a little man in Porchester Mews – a Pole, actually – and he does them beautifully. We've got several.' She tilted the sampler towards the light and gave a small, satisfied sigh. 'Well, that's another thing off my plate. What a relief.'

He was bored by their constant talking, but it no longer distracted him. He found he could shut out their chatter when he wanted to think of something else, and on several occasions he had not even heard what they said to him, and was accused of day-dreaming. That was not what it felt like, however; sometimes he did day-dream, particularly at school, and he knew how the mind drifted like gossamer away from what was being said, and you viewed things from above, like those sleeping dreams when you are flying. But this was something different, for he felt more entirely detached, as if he were in another place, with other people. It was a curiously comforting sensation.

'Do you know,' said Venetia Walker, pinching the front of her blouse and shaking it, 'I do believe it's getting hotter every day. I'm *roasting.*'

There was no chance of him slipping out. His father still

insisted that he stay with the three women, and they did not appear to be interested in leaving the lodge, so he was pleasantly surprised when he heard Rosemary Cooper suggesting they go for a drive. He withdrew from his reverie and stopped doodling in the margins of his book.

'The thing is,' Rosemary went on, 'Michael's taken the shooting-brake.'

'There's Bobby's'.

Alice looked back at them narrowly. 'You know I don't drive.'

'Well then,' said Venetia, laughing, 'we'll just have to take the Healey. I'm sure Richard wouldn't mind if we took it for a spin. Just this once – and I know exactly where he keeps the keys.' She checked herself abruptly, and Rosemary looked away.

'I'm not sure if that's altogether wise,' she murmured doubtfully, but Venetia's enthusiasm was fired.

'Oh, do let's. It would be such fun. Blow away all the cobwebs. We could go tweeding.'

In the end, it was a choice between visiting the gardens at Dunallan, or going further north to the stones at Callanish. They told James to decide, and he chose the latter, because it would mean a longer trip away from Graeval, and he had always found gardens boring.

Now that it was agreed upon, they all seemed in a great hurry to be off, and even Alice in her glum way looked pleased.

'There's a guidebook on one of these shelves, somewhere,' she said. 'I'll see if I can find it. We don't want to get lost.'

Venetia peered teasingly at her. 'Why not?' she asked. 'It might be fun.'

She had clearly not driven the car before, and took them down the drive at great speed in first gear. 'Hold on tight,' she cried, as they swung out into the road with a great jolt to the suspension.

Even with the front windows open, the inside of the car was hot and made him feel slightly sick as he watched the landscape pouring past.

. . . . .

She smoothed away at the mossy hump, speaking gently with a reassuring smile, like a nurse lulling a child in the cradle. No wind disturbed the wild and scattered vegetation beneath the walls; the odd, still stalk of coarse barley stood stiffly, and even the willow-herb was unstirring under the sheer light of the morning.

From her handkerchief the old woman unwrapped three brittle fragments of charred peat, now hard and cold, and crumbled them over the small mound, spreading them into a thin dark blanket with her palms.

'*Mo chubhrachan,*' she whispered, whirring, '*is cuimhue leam e.*' The memory of it is still upon me.

There was a soft look of satisfaction in her eyes, and she lightly kissed the dry earth. '*Cadal fada ri gaoith mhoir.*'

A long sleep in a big wind.

. . . . .

'Are we nearly there?' wondered Rosemary, as the car looped and swung along the narrow coastal road. 'It all looks most unlikely.'

They were skirting numerous inlets and sea-lochs, the dreary open track of moorland stretching away inland to their left. It was almost two hours since they had left the lodge, but Alice was insistent they were on the right route.

'It should be coming up quite soon,' she said, consulting her book.

'This had better be worth it when we get there,' said Rosemary. 'What on earth could have given anyone the idea of building a temple out here? I mean, who was it meant for in the first place?'

Alice was looking groggy, and shook her head. 'I can't

read any more when we're going this fast. You'll just have to wait until we've stopped.'

When they drove over the crest and down towards Loch Roag, they all looked disappointed. 'But there's hardly anything there,' complained Venetia, 'that can't be it.' They parked in the little lay-by and stared at the huddle of broken-looking rocks.

'What does it say?' demanded Rosemary. 'What are we meant to be seeing?'

'Well,' replied Alice, scrutinising the page, 'the gist of it is that the standing stones are second in importance only to Stonehenge, and, well . . . nobody seems quite to know how old they are. Megalithic', she said, enunciating carefully, 'but their original purpose is unknown.'

'What a place,' said Venetia. 'It's crazy.'

'There are various legends concerning the stones of Callanish, which are sometimes known as the False Men,' Alice continued, rather enjoying her role as the provider of information, 'and the generally accepted theory is that they were associated with the old religion of the druids.'

They were now approaching the main circle up an avenue, where nine or ten stones remained, sticking up like old teeth. Unlike the others, the boy was fascinated. He had read stories about Stonehenge, although he had never been there, and about the pyramids, and Easter Island. How was it that so little was known about them; and what had happened to the stones that were missing? He ran on ahead of the others and into the broken circle where now only twelve stones remained upright, splintery looking shards of undressed gneiss embedded at lopsided angles.

'Thank heavens for some fresh air, at last,' breathed Alice. Her face, which had yellowed during the drive, was now recovering its accustomed pallor. 'There's a chambered cairn, it says, in the middle.'

'I expect that will be very interesting,' said Venetia, rolling her eyes.

There were mossy spines on them, and lichens like dabs of ash. The tallest one was maybe three times his own height and, as he looked up at its irregular apex, he suddenly found himself looking directly into the sun.

. . . . .

Giving a short groan, she dropped the ladle and it clattered down on to the hearth. As quickly as she could, Miss Mackenzie felt her way along the edge of the table and fell back into her chair, one hand clamped across her eyes.

She appeared to be in pain, shaking her head from side to side, and sweat was starting from her dried skin. '*Obh, obh . . . a Sheumais!*' she moaned, '*de rinn thu?*' What have you done?

After several moments of agitation, she dropped both hands into her lap and snapped her head up quite violently and stared directly at the wall in front of her. She was breathing deeply and heavily, her mouth open.

'*De tha sin a-muigh air a' mhuir?*' she said, her voice low.

What is that out on the sea?

. . . . .

He could hear one of them calling for him, but he was dazzled completely and could see only the burning after-image of the sun wobbling and glaring like a balloon full of liquid before him. James staggered and stretched out his hand to lean against the rough stone, but he pitched forward and felt a blow on the side of his head. It made the pulsating orange jolt suddenly into green and there was what sounded like a shout in his ear.

When his vision had cleared he realised something was wrong. He was lying not in the main circle, but some yards away, in a slight dip where some smaller, crumbling stones were scattered in a crater of scarred peat. He scrambled to his feet, and heard his name being called, though as if from the distance.

'Here,' he shouted 'here I am – over here.' But there was no longer anybody in the circle.

Puzzled, he made his way back up the incline, and looked all around him. There was bird-song high in the air, and he thought he could hear a cuckoo.

'James, James,' came a woman's voice again, but he could not see from where. The place seemed deserted, and he felt a quick clot of fear in his throat. The voice seemed to come from above him, and he looked up, only to be blinded once more by the sun.

When he came round, he was lying at the base of the tallest stone, his head cradled in Rosemary Cooper's skirted lap. His right temple was ringing with a dull pain, and he felt unbearably hot.

'Oh God, is he all right?' said Alice, hovering at an angle towards the edge of his vision.

The boy stirred and gave out a groan. 'Where am I?' he asked, confused.

Rosemary stroked his forehead with the warm tips of her fingers. 'You fell,' she said soothingly, 'that's all. It's all right now. Let's get you on your feet and back to the car.'

He walked slowly down the avenue with them. 'I got dazzled,' he explained, 'and wandered away somewhere.' He saw Alice frowning at him, and he decided to leave it at that. He had no idea how it happened, but he did not want to talk about it any more.

'It's this heat,' declared Venetia, fanning herself as she started the engine, 'it will be the death of us all.'

They settled him into the front seat, and he closed his eyes gratefully. His head ached, and he could feel the bump of the bruise hardening, though the skin was not broken. The journey back to Graeval passed largely in silence, and the women seemed subdued; even Venetia's driving had lost its enthusiasm.

When they got in, he went up to his room and lay down and slept, but he still felt disoriented when he awoke. Dr

Willis came up and sympathised with him before dinner, and pronounced there was no harm done, but he should take it easy.

'Very mild concussion, old chap. Rotten luck. Head a bit sore, I shouldn't wonder?'

James did not eat much of his meal, and went back to his bed directly it was over. When he closed his eyes tightly, the sun-print with its bright whorl of colour came back again, as if the heat had somehow actually entered his head. He turned and turned queasily on the pillow, unable to sink into sleep.

'I can't understand it,' Rosemary said to her husband, 'one minute he was trotting ahead, then, he just keeled over. Dazzled, I suppose.'

Alice Paton leaned across the table and raised a finger at her. 'That child,' she said, 'is very confused.'

'Maybe so,' his father replied, 'but when I was his age, I was always crashing into things. It's part of growing up.'

'It's the heat,' said Venetia once again, for the benefit of the men, 'it will be the death of us all.'

He dozed fitfully for hours, his knees tucked up against his belly. He heard the others come up the stairs, doors closing on the dark, their footsteps muffled through the walls.

James listened to the faint noise of the sea sucking on the shore, and the galleon creak of the floorboards as the house drifted to sleep.

XV

The weather had turned around during the night, and when he woke up his bedroom curtains were swaying and sighing back and forth across the carpet, swelling and stiffening like sails. The noise that was blown through the open window was different to what he had become used to hearing each morning, less regular and more crowded. A brisk wind was coming off the sea, scattering the cries of the birds and breaking the rhythm of the waves. He lay and listened to it glancing around the angles of the lodge and singing through the long, broken gutters.

'Well, this is more like it,' said Willis, rubbing his hands keenly. 'At least we'll have a decent scent.'

'Thank heavens we will all be able to breathe again,' said Rosemary Cooper, stroking the rim of her cup. 'And the midges will be gone. You know, I might even come out with you today.'

Already, there was a current of new feeling amongst them. Now that the suffocating heat had been blown away, they were more relaxed and enthusiastic and began talking more rapidly to each other. The boy was delighted the staleness had disappeared, especially when his father, newly benevolent in his heavy tweeds, said he no longer need confine himself to the lodge.

'Just be sure, though, that you are back in time for luncheon. We're on the home beat today, so we'll all meet back here, one o'clock sharp.'

It was surprisingly cold as he walked along the sand. The night winds had thrown up a white mass of cloud that was calving over the horizon like an iceberg, allowing the sun to break through for a few seconds at a time. Its fugitive light swept along the dark waves and up across the tangled surface of the moor where sheep were huddled in against the peat banks.

Around the headland, each skerry and tortoise-like outcrop was leaping with spray as the waves flew up against them and shattered. James scrambled over the slippery cassocks of weed, their little bladders making a soft popping sound under his boots. The wind bellowed in his ears as he stood on the promontory and watched the sea-birds whirling through the air.

Rachel Mackenzie greeted him rather quietly, with a frown rather than her usual smile; he wondered if he had disturbed her at an inconvenient time, because she seemed very busy with her basins and pans and was moving around the table with a speed he had not seen in her before.

'No, no, Seumas,' she assured him, wiping her hands on her long apron, 'you must surely come in, and be seated in your chair here, where it is ready for you.'

He did as he was invited, and she came clockwise around the table and stood before him looking seriously at his head. 'And whatever is it you've done to yourself,' she demanded, 'that you've the bump like a gull's egg on your skin there?' She stretched out a palm and covered his temple for a moment. It was the first time she had actually touched him, and her hand felt warm and surprisingly soft.

James told her he had fallen, on a stone.

'Well, you take more care. There's been accidents sufficient already for the island.'

'Oh, it's nothing. I'd forgotten about it actually.' His head still ached slightly, but he affected the habitual stoicism that was required at school.

'The head of a man is precious,' said Miss Mackenzie sternly, and began to pour tea. She handed him a mug, and a warm farl of oatmeal cake. 'Had you the drink taken your-self, then?' she asked. He looked at her blankly, until her face softened, and gave a dry laugh, and sat down opposite him.

'It's amazing,' said James. 'The whole place looks different when the sun goes in.'

'Aye, there's the weather changed now, as it had to. And it may be that's the last we'll feel of any heat until the long winter's done.' She sighed, and rubbed the back of her hand.

'I suppose it must get awfully cold,' he agreed, though he still couldn't imagine the landscape, fixed in his mind as bright and burned, really turning white with snow.

'The sun disappears,' she told him, 'and the dead months come, *miosan marbh*, and dark it is until ten of the morning.' She sipped her hot drink and looked at him. 'Aye, and we've the snow sometimes, but it's a rare thing to see its stripes along Graeval. Mostly it's the frost that puts a diamond light on the rocks with their winter jewellery, and there's the blue shadow even at noon. When the white snow comes it is that thick it lies along the sand of the shore, right up to the mouth of the water, where the cream of the wave sinks into it. And the island is quiet for a time, and very peaceful it is then, though you've to be busy fetching buckets of it in for melting into water, and no time to be resting. But usually there is only the cold knife of the wind, and the brown *muir*, in the dead months of the year.'

The boy conjured a picture of the hills covered in snow, unmarked and unvisited, like rooms newly painted and locked. White feet, white hands in the night. He nibbled at the coarse crumble of the oatcake, remembering the curious pleasure he had felt, as he trudged to chapel after a night of snowfall, at his first sight of the school grounds stretching away from the little wood, the scarred mud covered and level and bright. Later there had been the snowball matches against the prefects during which, one year, it was whispered, a boy named Sykes had lost an eye. By the end of the afternoon, the playing-fields were once more a mass of churned brown, with the monotonous imprint of studs.

'This last year, so it happened, there was scarcely a cold

159

breath to the air all winter,' continued the woman, 'which was a strangeness, but welcome just the same. Those that had to could walk out even after it was dark, with no fear of the cold bringing a man harm. Well, Seumas, that was never a thing I could remember before in all my life; but there was one *Leodhasach*, a person in Lewis, wrote in the newspaper that it was all the cause of an old saying: when there are three queens in Britain, winter shall become summer.' She chuckled at her tea and ducked her head. 'I would not have called it a summer exactly but I believe there were three living there all together, for a time.'

Perhaps it was something to do with this way she referred to things as if they were happening in some foreign country – it was difficult to say, but when Miss Mackenzie was speaking to him he enjoyed listening to her, even if he could not always understand the connections she did not explain. Nobody had ever spoken to James in this way before: when she told him things, she did not sound like a teacher or a parent, but gave him the impression that he was overhearing something private instead. It was almost like eavesdropping on someone thinking aloud. There were plenty of things that the people at the lodge talked about that he did not quite understand, but in those cases he simply found his mind wandering. The conversations at Graeval were quicker, and seemed to slide over the surface of things with a rapid, rattling noise, and the words seldom lingered in his mind, and they carried no pictures to his eye.

'What do you do then?' he asked. 'Do you just stay indoors all the time?' He wondered about food, and how you would get to see a doctor if you got ill with a cold. There wasn't even a telephone, in case you had an accident.

She held up a hand and shook it at him, as if he had mis-understood. 'It's earlier days I'm thinking on, before folk moved away, and the place was changed. There would always be the visiting in those days, never a person left alone – it was not the way, not then. We'd have the *ceilidh*, right enough,

and stories there were then sufficient to be told each night
excepting the Sabbath, when we would instead read from
the Book. But the gathering then, it was a proper thing, not
your manufactured party.' Her voice pronounced the adjec-
tive with slow contempt. 'When my father was living, now,
there'd come from miles away across the island to our hearth
– in the black house, there – people just to listen. *Bha e 'na
sheanchaidh.* He was the teller of tales, very respectable in
these islands.'

'What was he, a writer?'

The old woman left her chair and went and stood before
the fire. 'He surely was not,' she said, fetching something
down from her wooden mantelpiece, 'for he could no more
write than the rest of his father's family. No, no. He had the
histories of the island right in his heart, where he remembered
them on the behalf of everyone that lived here.'

She came back to the table. 'It was a gift,' she explained
simply.

There was a stubby pipe of yellowed clay on her palm. It
had been broken and mended in two places along the stem,
and there were dry brown cracks at the joins.

'And this was his,' she said, 'for there would be nothing of
a tale to be had before he had set a flame to his snush of
tobacco, and then we'd wait until the smoke was drawing,
and he'd begin. Sometimes a dozen of us listening there, and
you could never know for certain what would be the subject
until he'd begun. It's gone now, the *ceilidh*, but it was that
brightened the long nights of winter, when we'd not even a
lamp to see our knitting by, but only the skarts for candles,
dried sea-birds with a wick pulled through their grey car-
casses.'

James turned the little pipe around in his hands. It still had
the rough smell of tobacco about it. 'It must be very old,' he
said, appreciating it.

A brittle expression came into her face as she took it back.
'Aye, it's old enough, and he'd never be doing with a new

one. For every time that it would break, while he was out in his boat on the sea, he'd mend it with a drop or two of blood from the back of his finger, and so preserve it. To him it was an old thing that was precious.' She replaced it over the fire.

As she shuffled back towards her chair, he was aware of another sound, somewhere around him in the house, like a hollow dripping. James turned around in his seat, but both of the taps in the basin were dry. It continued, slow and steady, but he could see nothing that might be causing it.

Miss Mackenzie did not appear to notice. 'But there's hardly a person visits this house any more,' she said, though without any sense of complaining. 'Which makes you, Seumas, the more welcome, so it does.' She flapped her hands at him, and he realised he was being paid a compliment. 'There's things happen that keep folk away,' she went on, 'and the island has seen changes, like the world itself. Everybody is in a hurry, and they've no time for listening, and there's few could understand if they wished to, for my father's tales, as I have them, are in the Gaelic, and it's now an English education that they're all needing.'

'But, I've understood all the stories you've told me,' he protested with a frown.

'Have you, Seumas *ban*? I would wonder if you had.' She was frowning back at him. She retrieved her cup and began drinking, her eyelids drooping with each gulp. '*Gaidhealtachd*, the kingdom of the Gael, it's a memory now in the minds of old women.'

The boy shook his head in sympathy. He had never heard of such a kingdom, but her look of disappointment was plain as she hunched there, brooding in the web of her memory.

'He would say, my father, that the language of the Gael was like the ivy on a wall, which is pulled away for spoiling the face of a building. But you'd find that down the long years it was that had been holding the house together.'

James shifted gently in his chair. It seemed she was wandering off into thoughts that he should not interrupt, but they made no immediate sense to him. He could see no way of excusing himself without embarrassment, but was worried about staying there, sitting too long while she rambled.

There was a slight pause, as she swallowed her mouthful of liquid, and then her eyes flicked up at him with a sudden directness. 'All that I have been saying does not matter, you need not mind the memories that I have, for they are of no importance. But soon you will be leaving the island, and now the weather has a change on it, you must understand what it means to us when the summer is over, for that is a particular day. May be it is today, there are few ways of knowing, but the life goes out of the island, and the tides run slow through the winter. When you are young, it carries no fears with it, for you understand that the sun will return, with you there to greet it – *an tobar nach traigh*, the fountain that does not dry up.'

She was losing him almost entirely; it had never occurred to him that the winter might be different for those who were old, except if they could not keep warm, and there was no one to look after them. Surely, everyone knew that the seasons returned in the same way each year? And there was always Christmas, and New Year, to celebrate. He could not quite see why she was looking so gloomy.

'There is an ending to winter, as there is to all things,' explained Miss Mackenzie, 'and I pray that I may be spared to see it once again, but there's no knowing. In the middle of the month called *Faoilleach*, the wolf month, that would be February, that's the day that the old ones are glad for when it comes, and seventy-nine of those I've been blessed to see. The thirteenth day of that month, the water in the sea runs warm, all but the last of the nine long waves that come cold from the heart of the ocean. And that we know as *Latha Brighde*, Bride's day, when she breathes her warmth into the mouth of the year, and lights the fires of our spring. The yellow flower appears like a spark on the hill, *Bearnan Brighde*, her little notched one. Your dandelion.'

It was becoming more difficult to keep up with her, and he realised he was staring at the woman's face without being able to say anything. He supposed she was talking about a special day when weddings were celebrated, but the whole thing seemed unlikely. Besides, her voice was rising in pitch very slightly the more she went on speaking to him.

'Eighty-eight years of age she had lived when she died, and was taken, on the eighth month of that year, in the *Cill Dara*, that cell where she lived in the middle of the oak. And a voice was heard, calling through the trees, "Arise, make haste my beautiful one, and come, for the Winter is now past." And she passed out of sight, though the flame was kept alive burning for her in the grove there for hundreds of years, to her memory.'

Gently rocking back and forth in her chair, Miss Mackenzie began to sing, in a brief, hard tone, '*Brighde-nan-Brat, Brighde-nan-Brat*,' her thin eyebrows arched, as if she were listening rather than chanting it to herself. The boy coughed artificially, but she continued until he asked her directly: 'When did that happen . . . I mean, who was the bride?' He was very much hoping he could bring this reverie to an end, or at least understand something of it. There was something a little frightening in the distant expression in Rachel Mackenzie's face, something he had seen before, in quite a different place, when trying to speak to his mother. It was the way that her eyes were narrowed, and concentrating, and looking above him, urgent but remote.

'Mary of the Gael,' whirred her voice, 'the foster-mother of the Christ, *Muime Chriosd*, and many were the wonders that she did, for she was a saint, a calm one and born at the sunrise as her mother returned from milking, on the threshold of the house, not inside nor outside, and daughter of a king of Ireland. This was the beginning of the prophecy, and some there are still believe it, for surely it was seen to be true. In a hot land, after a great falling of rain, the Prince of the world was to be born, and she travelled there – how, it was not understood – by night, and was at the stable, where she gave them ale and milk for the heat, and the waters came, and she wrapped him up in her mantle. She was the first to hold him in all the world.'

Now he could picture once again what she was referring to, a scene imprinted on his mind since he was a child, though he could not remember anything about a woman from Ireland at the Nativity. There was something rather exciting about it, all the same, if you took the idea quite literally.

'And when he was a man, and his enemies hunted him through these islands as they did, she sent her bird, *gille-Brighde*, the oyster-catcher, and he hid him under the weeds of the shore, and since that day of days the bird has the mark upon him, a cross on his side. And the noise that you hear him make says "Be wise. Be wise." '

James nodded enthusiastically, 'I think I've seen oyster-catchers,' he told her. She had grasped the arms of her chair as if to stand up, but she remained seated, her body taut and shuddering slightly. She was speaking high, now, like someone intoning.

'Fair she was, with brown hair, and wisdom upon her, but she would have no man for a husband. She knew the temptations of her beauty, and when she had lived for sixteen years she prayed aloud for some deformity to spoil her in the sight of men. When straight away upon the asking the left eye broke open in her head, and it melted.'

Miss Mackenzie stopped abruptly, shaking her head. She looked down at the surface of her table, and pressed her lips tightly together. The boy could hear the heavy depth of her breathing.

'And when she took the veil, her beauty was restored at that moment, and the wood of the altar where she knelt sent up green shoots. For the glory of it. Each spring, each spring she walks through the morning along our shore, with her birds piping before her, and you'd know her again for the beauty that's behind the world. For she hung her cloak upon a sunbeam.'

Huddling into her shawl once more, she regarded him as if uncertain whether to go on. The silence swelled around them, broken only by a noise of dripping.

When she resumed, the woman's voice was nasal, and thinner than he had ever heard from her before. 'There was a child,' she was saying, 'had the white fever, and in her sleep she saw a woman that came to the side of her bed, with a skin on her as pale as milk. She laid some sweet flowers by the head, and smoothed her with cool water, so that the comfort of it was beautiful. For it was Bride that was there, who brought the healing to these islands, and is blessed for it.'

He was alarmed when she stood suddenly up, and clutched at her right arm with her left hand. The boy leaned forward to see if he could help her, since she was obviously agitated, but she paid no attention to him.

' "*C'uin a thilleas tu,*
Oh mo ghradh?" '

said Miss Mackenzie, her voice soft as that of a child.

' "When will you come again, my dear one?" she said. But the Bride shook her head.' She slowly shook her own head in imitation.

' "*Cha till mi an rathad so;*
Tha an t-aite cumhang," '

was the reply she made – "I will not return this way, for the place is narrow." And, when her mother came to waken the child the next morning, she was greyer than a chill dawn.'

James surprised himself by speaking his thoughts out loud. 'That's awfully sad,' he said, 'did it really happen?' He found he could picture it perfectly.

The woman nodded. 'I had it from my father, and I believe it to be true.' She was now looking exhausted, as if parts of her face had begun to collapse slightly. He said goodbye to her, and went to open the door. Outside, it was raining.

It was still no more than a smurr on the wind like a fine spray, but evidently a great storm was collecting. There was already a new smell in the air, a dark, thick smell that the earth gave off as the hard rind of the moorland absorbed the long delayed water. He pulled up the hood of his anorak and set off as quickly as he could for the lodge.

The sky was shifting, massive and lurid overhead, the obscured sun straining through like a cyclamen bruise. He slipped twice on the rocks in his haste, and it was one o'clock before he reached the driveway at the end of which Graeval stood, damp and angular under the dark machinery of the clouds.

. . . . .

By the time they had finished their lunch, the glass in the windows facing the shore was bulging in and out with the gale. Beyond the flickering lawn, the sea was churning grey and white, spume from the wave-tops being blown as far as the lodge itself. Flurries of water hit the panes with the sound of earth being sieved.

'Thank God we weren't on the high ground,' said Benson through a cheekful of vegetables. 'The cars would never have made it back.'

'A proper old howler,' said Willis, looking happily out of the window.

They were visibly cheered by this sudden escalation in the weather, and only Bobby Paton, picking over his chop, looked morose. 'Too much, too late,' he pronounced drily. 'There'll be a dirty great spate for days after this little lot, though I expect the water will be just about perfect as we pack off south.'

James's father laughed with evident pleasure at this gloominess. 'Do stop moaning, Bobby. We'll have a fish out before we go, mark my words. I'm bloody well going to try tomorrow, whatever the experts say. There's always the lochs, after all.'

'The level will be up and down like a yo-yo,' countered Paton, 'the fish will be unsettled. Peat makes them sick, you know that.'

Benson winked at the others. 'There's always a Job in every crowd.'

'I'm afraid that I shall be proved correct, none the less.'

His wife looked at him sweetly. 'No doubt,' she said, sipping some wine.

For the first time a fire was lit in the drawing-room, and the place had an air of close comfort to it, like that of a wintry evening. James knelt on the window-seat and stared out at the rioting shore. Rain and spray came blashing sporadically against the glass, exploding his reflection. It was not like any storm he had experienced before; the noises were quite different, and with no trees or other houses nearby there was a sense of a long uninterrupted force bearing in on the lodge alone.

There was no question of anyone venturing out, and a leisurely, unhurried atmosphere prevailed. Cooper went off to decant more port, and the cards were produced for bridge. 'It's rather nice to feel one doesn't have to *do* anything,' Rosemary Cooper remarked as she settled before the fire with her magazine.

Despite occasional glances of lightning, there was no thunder. The electricity danced silently above the water and then went out, wiping away the details of the seascape and leaving in the gloom only the deep drumming of the wind, the ragged artillery of the surf.

'I only hope the roof is sound,' said Rosemary, 'or we shall all be sleeping in oilskins.'

He wondered if there would be a serious flood. Mr Luxmoore had told them that in really heavy storms there were millions of tons of water ready to fall over quite small areas. When it rained in the tropics you could scoop the fresh water off the surface of the sea, it was coming down so heavily. Perhaps Miss Mackenzie was right: they wouldn't see the sun again for a long time now.

'Aha, young James. Got something here might interest you,' said Willis, his voice thickened with port. 'Care to have a peek. Eh?' He was sitting at the table in the corner, unpacking the contents of a varnished wooden case. The boy went dutifully and looked over his shoulder. 'No time to be wasted, playing with cards, any of that tommy rot.' He rapped the box with his fingers. 'Got to get tying, you know, get out the old vice. There's fish in the offing. No time for fun and games.'

He was unpacking clutches of yellowed, translucent envelopes, distributing them in apparently random piles. Through the flimsy paper the boy could see sprays of feathers pressed flat with age, and little tangles of fish-hooks. From inside the case sprouted the tips of furry tails, plumes of peacock and golden pheasant, stray loops of silk spilling from various compartments.

'You just watch me,' blurted the doctor, 'I'll steal a march on that father of yours, that's a racing cert. You see if I don't.' He tapped the wing of his nose. 'Tie up a few killers while their backs are turned, stock up for the morrow. You stick with me, young fellow: we'll knock 'em into a cocked hat. Make a good team, eh? What d'you say?' He nudged the boy confidentially. 'Look at this now, this little beauty.' Willis held up a small, waxy feather that looked as if an eye had been painted on it.

'That's a good one,' said James, trying to enter into the conspiracy. 'What is it?'

Dr Willis chuckled at him and nodded, his breath plumed with drink. 'Jungle cock. Ssh! Need it for my secret weapon, you see. Call it the General Surgeon.'

'I don't know who you think you're fooling,' Bobby Paton cut in, 'but we can all hear you loud and clear.'

'You'll be sorry,' said Willis, 'you'll be wanting one tomorrow, but they're not for sale.' His voice dropped once more. 'These General Surgeons,' he repeated. 'As my colleagues say, they're all killers!'

He laughed immensely at his joke, and the boy laughed along with him, because Dr Willis was a funny man and though he did not understand the joke, the others never took him seriously, so it was safe to laugh.

The wind was yawning noisily down the chimney, sending spurts of peat-smoke into the room. The fire was steeply banked, its crest a turban of flames.

'Scarlet Ibis,' declared Willis, twirling a bright feather under the lamp, and grunting in appreciation. 'Now, that's a rare one. Don't suppose you can get it any more. Chap gave me a whole body skin before the war. God knows how he came by it. Jolly useful, all the same.'

Michael Cooper returned with a decanter and sat himself down in front of the fire. He had several envelopes in his hand, and began to tear them open, his feet up on the fender.

'Just you watch,' muttered Willis, 'just you watch.'

'Whatever is it, darling?' enquired Rosemary. Her husband had sprung to his feet and was thrusting a sheet of paper at her, cigar smoke heaving around his face.

'I simply do not believe it,' he burst out. 'It's Tony Straker. Well, read it.' He hit the letter with the back of his hand and turned away. 'The idiot! The man's a total, bloody idiot!' He was pacing along the rug, smoothing repeatedly at his oiled hair.

The others looked up in concern. 'I don't understand,' said Rosemary quietly. 'What is all this about?' She ran her eyes along the letter with an expression of great scrutiny, shaking her head. 'I'm not sure I quite understand.'

Michael Cooper pointed at the letter like a man producing evidence. 'Last week,' he explained heatedly, 'last week I told him to sell short with a huge holding of stock. And what do I find? He's still sitting on it. We've missed the swing. The market's peaked, and we've missed it. The man's mad.'

'Well, maybe he never got your letter,' she replied, trying to reassure him. 'There's no mention of it here.' She smiled, relieved at having found a solution. 'Yes, that's all it is surely?'

'*All?*' he said throatily. 'It could have netted me thousands. I'm telling you. Why can't he bloody well do as he's told? Everybody else has to. I mean, *thousands.*' He stomped over and sloshed more port into his glass.

'It might have gone astray, darling; it does sometimes happen,' she said, leaning forward in concern.

He closed his eyes. 'God damn it,' he said wearily. 'If only I'd been there myself.'

James looked into the fire where the envelope was rattling into flame. He wondered if the winds would ever be strong enough to uncover the letters he had buried at the back of the dunes.

. . . . .

There was a paraffin lamp by her bed, its wick turned up high. It was the only light in the house, as the fire in the hearth had gone out completely. She had wrapped herself in blankets, a hot stone water-bottle clutched to her belly.

'*De 'm faileadh tha sin?*' she said, her voice a dry hiss. What is that smell?

She was hugging herself, and shaking on the bed, her face a clench of pain. It was not just the cold that was making her teeth clatter; her eyes were streaming, and she was clearly in the grip of a fever.

In the thick shell of her house the noise of the rain was muted, loud only at the windows, but from inside there echoed the sound of water dripping slowly. Outside, the thunder began shaking its sheet as the storm escalated, but she was not listening to that. Short, grating noises rasped from her throat, and she shivered, clutching her forearms.

'*Se sin faileadh dhitheanan.*'

It is the smell of flowers.

. . . . .

171

By five the sky was dark as a night, and three of the men were dozing. Geoffrey Willis still fumbled with his threads and fur, but the materials he was fastening to the hook-shanks were increasingly misshapen and untidy, and his eyelids were converging slowly from the port.

There was scarcely any noise from within the room except the long sighs of the men breathing, and the click and clack coming from the blades of the fire. James had sunk into his enjoyment of the afternoon by pretending to read, while actually concentrating on the flames that dominated the room, and thinking up stories about the fire.

He imagined what it must have been like to be burned at the stake. He remembered reading that most of the victims were suffocated by the smoke before they felt any pain, but even now his knees were uncomfortably hot some feet away from the blaze, and he didn't see how that would ever have been possible. If you had to choose between freezing to death and burning to death, he wondered, which would be better? One Roman man, a hero, had apparently thrust his hand into a flame to prove he wasn't a liar.

It spat and clattered in the grate, spiralling under the draught. Where did the yellow come from, and that odd flash of green?

'Oh, fuck,' grunted Willis, his dropped bobbin unreeling along the floor.

Had there really been a great forest fire on the island? The boy's mind conjured a picture of Magnus Bareleg, standing in the prow of a long boat, one foot on the rim, one leg bare from the knee down, thick with muscle. He held a short, curved sword in one hand and he was approaching a beach where a group of figures was crouching in fear on the sand.

He hurled a firebrand, a torch, high out in an arc over the water. The dense trees behind the people began to go up, one by one.

It was a long time since he'd settled so happily in front of a fire. When he was younger, and they'd all been together for the Christmas holidays, he used to curl up on the sofa in front of the little fire-place in his mother's room, wrapped in his woolly dressing-gown until his short, gleaming hair dried out, just listening to her read. She had a thick story-book, bound in dark blue cloth, with a coloured picture of an old shoe-maker on the front. She would imitate the different voices – the Basket-woman, Baba Yaga, the Lost Child, Balder the Beautiful; but it was no use thinking of that now. He was far away, a different person.

At the time, people had said it was incredible, and even now he did not quite believe it. His father had told him some-thing quite different, of course, but he had realised at once that that was not the truth. You didn't get sent to a hospital just for shop-lifting.

It was Guy Walker who told him what had happened. One day, during the sales, she was supposed to have attacked an-other woman. That was the story, and he clearly remembered the name that Walker must have invented for her – Mrs Matheson from Weybridge, he said she was called. There had been a dispute about a set of kitchen pans, and afterwards his mother had been taken away, and since that day, more than a year ago, he had not seen her.

Walker had enjoyed telling him, but he was making some of it up. He said his mother had cut off two of Mrs Matheson's fingers with a serrated carving-knife.

The fire glugged steadily in the grate, with the noise of distant trains going over sleepers.

XVI

For two days it rained, then a dawn came up yellow and grey, the sun looking pale and distant in the mouth of the horizon. The wind had softened but still it was strong, sending irregular showers shivering across the sea and the damaged faces of the sand.

Inside the lodge there was a general sense of exhaustion. The generator had failed twice, and the foretaste of cold coupled with the relentless rattling of the rain had left them all unsettled. The novelty of the wild weather had soon given way to a feeling of monotonous siege, and a reminder of the uncomfortable conditions that had prevailed across the country in recent years. It threatened to cast a gloom over their holiday, if it persisted.

'Well, this is definitely better,' pronounced Benson, his hand rising over the breakfast table and gesturing towards the window, as if introducing a newcomer. 'I don't know about all of you, but I'm fed up with kicking my heels, and time, as they say, is of the essence. I'm going fishing.'

Willis nodded vigorously, gobbling at his buttery bap. 'Count me in, Richard. I'm your man.'

'I've had a word with Grant, and he reckons there might be a chance on the river – no more than that. I propose, if there are no objections, that Venetia and I give it a try this morning. I'd love her to catch a fish. What do you think?'

There was no mention, James noticed, of his father's previous desire that he should catch a salmon.

'You can count us out for starters,' said Paton. 'I see no sense in getting wet for nothing, and with all this water coming down the fish will be uncatchable. It's an academic exercise.'

His wife gave him a sly smile. 'Oh well, then,' she agreed, 'if there's no sense in it, Bobby, I don't think we should take the risk. Do you?'

'You go if you so wish. But you know perfectly well what I mean.'

James was pleased when he heard that Alec was back on duty again. There was some debate, however, about whether his leg would be strong enough to hold a boat in the wind, and finally it was agreed that he would be confined to the river while Grant took James and Dr Willis out on the loch. The two parties would report to the others on their success over lunch.

Willie Grant was standing outside the gun-room, hands on his hips, studying the sky with the self-important look of a professional. 'Aye, laddie; ye'll be needing all your buttons the day,' he told James as the boy ran out into the yard, fastening his duffle. The clouds boiling overhead were still dark enough in places. 'That's to be a wetting rain yet,' nodded the keeper.

James pulled on the thick knitted hat he had been given, rough and prickly over the tips of his ears.

Leaning against the far corner of the table was Alec, dressed once again in his long oiled coat. He was staring down at the floor, one boot chafing idly at the leg of the table, and he did not look up as James came hurrying in.

'Hello,' said the boy eagerly. 'I'm glad you're better.'

Alec mumbled a greeting and shifted his stance. He began to fiddle with the metal fly-boxes that were spread on the table before him, opening each one in turn as if intent on a last minute inspection of their contents.

'Do you think we'll get one?'

'I'm not saying, Master James. I've not had my instructions yet.'

The boy was astonished at this new way he was being treated. It occurred to him that he must have done something wrong, offended Alec in some way, but before he could say

175

anything further they were interrupted by the busy arrival of Geoffrey Willis, his waterproofs rustling.

'Morning Campbell. Glad to see you up and about again. Feeling steady on your pins? Splendid, splendid.' He stood across the table from the other man and began rubbing his large hands together noisily.

'I am much improved, Doctor, thank you.' He managed a polite smile, but still did not look directly at the boy. 'Every day a little better.'

'That's the idea. Well,' said Willis, 'we're off to Craiggie, so it seems. No time to lose. Tight lines to you.'

Alec stood to attention. 'And the same to you, Doctor.' He caught James's eye as he looked up. 'Both of you,' he added briskly. 'Both of you.'

The Land Rover began to churn its way up the track that ran beside the river, its wipers reaping the morning rain. As they proceeded, in a series of harsh bounces, Willis was struggling to extract from his various pockets the spools and scissors, tins and wallets without which his foray against the fish of Loch Craiggie would be to no avail. He gathered his bits of equipment together, checking them and feeling each item as if for reassurance that nothing had happened to alter their familiarity since the last time they had been summoned to his help.

He brandished a bright fly, bristling with feathers, under the keeper's nose. 'Look here,' he announced, 'the General Surgeon! Never seen one like that before, eh, Grant?'

The man was wrestling the wheels through the peaty sludge, and took his eye off the streaming track just long enough to have a squint at the proffered lure. 'Aye, that'd be a topper, sir. Just the boy.'

Willis slapped James happily on the thigh. 'Hear that, young Benson? Hear what the expert says? What do you reckon – five by lunch-time?'

'Each,' suggested Willie Grant, 'else I'm not rowing to shore.' As they wound their way along, he maintained a smooth commentary about how the sport at Graeval had

176

improved since he first arrived there. It was a shame, he told them, that the estate was so rarely taken by experienced sportsmen, for it had the potential to be among the best in the islands, but it was not every day that he could count on gentlemen like those in Mr Benson's party. He was very hopeful, he said, that they would be returning next year, when the weather was sure to be more favourable, and he'd have to order a new game-book to fit in all the entries.

Their boots sank into the thick fudgy peat as they squelched down to where the boat was pulled up. It had not been launched all season, and the footboards were floating on several inches of rainwater. The bailer, a ribbed catering tin, bobbed around next to the bright curl of its label which had soaked off after a summer of being baked on to the metal. It was now the consistency of glue, sodden and on the point of disintegration: Australian Cling Peaches, it read. They bailed it overboard with the water and its drowned insects.

They had nothing when they arrived back for lunch. 'Not a sausage!' announced Willis, as he clambered from the car. 'You?'

James's father had taken off his jacket and was smoking a cigar in the yard. He was clearly pleased about something, and the two returning anglers looked at each other in sympathy. 'You'd better come and have a look,' he called, beckoning them inside.

'Gosh!' said the boy, reaching out at once to touch the largest one, 'did you catch them all?' Under the sprinkler lay three dead salmon on the slab.

'As it happens, I did not,' came the reply. Benson nudged open the green swing door and called, 'Darling.' A moment later there came the striking sound of sharp heels on the stone hall, and Venetia Walker appeared from the dining-room, a glass of wine in her hand. Her face was thickly smeared with fish blood, which looked like war-paint around her smile.

'Well, Grant, her first fish. Hooked and landed all on her own. What do you say?' He put one arm around her shoulders and hugged her proudly.

The head keeper came respectfully forward and congratulated her, shaking her by the hand, but his voice was distinctly flat. 'I had that feeling, madam, the river might be the place to try. And see how well you've done.' It was Alec, after all, who had actually been in attendance, and Willie Grant withdrew as quietly as possible in search of his lunch.

'What did we tell you, Bobby?' said James's father with a look of teasing triumph. 'Nothing ventured, and all that.' He was relishing the situation, and was drinking rather quickly.

Paton gave him a demure nod. 'I'm amazed. But I concede that I may have been wrong.'

'Did you hear that?' asked Alice, looking around the table. 'That makes two of us who are amazed.'

Plans for the afternoon's sport were being rapidly discussed, and the men were setting out their various theories about the mysterious behaviour of the fish, why they should be caught in one place but not in another, what made salmon take an artificial fly when it was common knowledge they did not feed in fresh water. Michael Cooper told a rather cumbersome story about an uncle of his who, at the end of a fruitless day flogging a river, hurled his fly-box into the pool and saw it swallowed up by a gigantic salmon.

'I'm rather inclined to think,' Dr Willis told Rosemary, 'that it is all something to do with the phases of the moon. One might look into it, maybe write a book on the subject. It's perfectly intriguing, don't you agree?'

Venetia Walker laid a hand on his arm. 'You know what I think, Geoffrey?' she asked him throatily. 'I think it's all a matter of luck. No, I do. We just happened to be in the right place. If it wasn't for Campbell, I doubt we'd have done any better than you. Honestly.'

'Oh, can you beat it,' exclaimed James's father, waving his unlit cigar. 'How typically feminine! That beggar did nothing but lean sulkily on his gaff all morning, and suddenly he's one of the Wise Men.'

She was enjoying her position, however, and refused to be

browbeaten. Ignoring Benson's remarks, she addressed herself to the other women, as if the three of them were alone. 'Of course, Richard wasn't even in sight half the time; went striding away down the bank, ignoring the poor man's advice altogether. Campbell was emphatic about the Long Pool, or whatever it was, but Izaak Walton there knew a better place, as usual.'

James watched his father's face go tense, though he was still smiling. 'I got two to your one, as it turned out. So I think that rather proves my point, does it not?' He winked affably at Cooper.

'If a new girl like me could catch one,' concluded Venetia, 'who knows what vast numbers the Head Boy might have caught, if he'd done what he was told.'

'It is not the purpose of a ghillie to tell his rod what to do,' objected Paton irritably, 'but to be on hand to land the fish. Personally, I shouldn't pay the blindest bit of attention to what Campbell has to say. He's only looking for a dram when he offers advice. One would be better off on one's own like Richard was.'

But as they filed out into the hall, Willie Grant was standing just inside the little office, his deer-stalker in his hand. He explained that there was a slight impediment to the afternoon's arrangements, because the under-keeper was no longer free to accompany them.

'Well, what is it this time?' demanded Paton, who by now had set his heart on killing some fish. 'He's been off for a week as it is.'

The tone of apology that shaded Grant's reply suggested he was in agreement with their indignation. 'It's a relative of his, sir, an old aunt. She's taken a turn, and there's a doctor down from Stornoway. She was not discovered until this morning. But we shall manage all right, gentlemen.' He beamed at them reassuringly.

'What seems to be the problem?' asked Willis. 'Is there something I can do to help?'

'Ach, no, Doctor; I wouldn't be putting yourself out when there's fish to be caught. Dr Graham's attending, and he's used to the sickness in this area.'

Geoffrey Willis began to pack his pipe methodically. 'Maybe so, but it must be serious if it requires Campbell to absent himself from his duties. Have you any idea what is wrong?'

'That I couldna say, Doctor; it might be anything. She's a mad old lady, lives on her own. It is probable she took a fall.'

'Very well. But it will do no harm if I pop down and make my number with my colleague in arms. Professional courtesy, you understand. Just point me in the right direction, and I'll join you all at the water.'

'You're a saint,' Rosemary Cooper assured him, knotting her headscarf in front of the mirror.

'Saint Geoffrey of Graeval,' said Benson, 'who denied himself fish during a flood.'

'I'm a doctor,' Willis said, a little offended. 'Not a very good one, perhaps, but there we go.' He pulled on his cap and made for the yard. 'Have no fear, I will beat you all at the end of the day.'

While this had been happening, the boy had remained standing behind his father, silent with concern over the vagueness of the news. But now, on impulse, he darted forward towards the green door and said, 'Hang on. I'll come with you.'

Willis turned. 'Why on earth would you want to do that?'

James looked up at him and realised it was not the moment to talk about Miss Mackenzie. There was nothing he could actually do, and it would only lead to endless questions. He shrugged, as if baffled at himself. 'I don't know,' he said lamely, 'I thought you might like me to.' He felt useless and confused, as if he had betrayed the old woman when he might have helped her.

So it was that he went to the river to spend the afternoon fishing, and caught a salmon, and they slit the gill of the dead fish and wiped a dark clot of blood over his face, and no one could quite understand why he wasn't delighted.

Later, as they waited for the gong that would summon them down to dine, the boy listened to Geoffrey Willis as he told the women about his visit. He started off by describing how he had lost his way, and made them laugh in his usual fashion by imitating his surprise at driving the car into a sheep-dipping fank that he mistook for a lay-by. But the boy could see in a way more clearly than he ever had before that Dr Willis was just playing up to them, and there was something harder underneath his jolly account, something he was hoping to avoid saying.

It was Alice Paton who punctured his performance. 'But, Geoffrey, don't keep us in suspense too long. What was wrong with her? What on earth was the emergency all about?'

'Yes,' nodded Rosemary, her hands clasped in concern, 'that's what has been worrying us.'

'Well, the old dear had some kind of seizure, left her in a bit of a state. Can't say I'm entirely surprised, mind you: the place she lives in is perishingly cold, no electricity of course, and there's no saying how long she'd been lying there. Graham's a solid fellow, though, a Bart's man, would you believe? Wanted to take her straight up to the hospital for observation, but she wasn't having that. All she could do to make herself understood, in fact – slight paralysis of the facial muscles, you see, but quite common in such cases. Campbell's going to drive her up tomorrow morning, I believe, for some tests.'

The gong thrummed and they made their way down the stairs.

'It strikes me as unforgivable,' Paton told him while the soup was being served, 'that a woman of that age – what was she, eighty? ninety? – should be allowed to live in a remote cottage entirely on her own when she has younger members of her family living quite comfortably in the same community.' He frowned at his slender glass of sherry, and tipped some into his broth. 'She should be in a home, at the very least. So much for the Highland spirit. What kind of a society is it that leaves a pensioner unvisited during a two-day storm – good God, this isn't Russia.'

He caught sight of James staring at him over a raised spoon. 'You probably don't know what I'm talking about,' Paton told him, turning away to address the others, 'but we have so much rammed down our throats today about traditional lifestyles, and maintaining the values of communities. All arguments against progress. And what happens when you look at it closely? The places in question are just bloody primitive, and I can't see the sense in perpetuating that.'

'Care of the elderly is a difficult thing,' said Willis cautiously, 'it varies from place to place, you know, and sometimes they're happier being left to their own devices. Within reason.'

'Still on about your latest patient?' asked Benson, from the head of the table.

'What's that? Well, yes, I suppose we were. You know . . .'

'I've a little bit of background information about the Campbell woman that might interest you. Care to hear it?'

'Her name's Mackenzie,' said Willis.

'Whatever. Something I heard from Grant while we were in the boat this afternoon. Difficult to believe, perhaps, in this day and age, but here it goes. The reason that nobody visits her is quite simple: they think she's got second sight. As popular as leprosy up here, apparently: the islanders won't touch her with a bargepole. They're convinced of it.' He pointed his fork at the doctor. 'There. What do you make of that?'

There was a thick stirring as several people spoke at once, but above it all the opinion of Bobby Paton rose with satisfaction. 'It doesn't surprise me in the least. That's just what I've been saying all along.' His eyes danced across from left to right. 'Primitive beyond all comprehension. Voodoo stuff. The dark ages. Call it what you will. It's like dealing with a bunch of colonials.'

182

'You're a fool,' his wife interrupted, staring at her empty bowl. 'You're all the same. Do you have the faintest idea,' she asked him, her voice high and clear, 'the damage you do when you say things like that? When you deliberately say things like that?'

The subject was quickly changed to a discussion of the weather, and from that they drifted reluctantly on to details of the different routes they would have to take on the journey south. When the meal was over, James went upstairs straightaway, without going through the formal rituals of saying good-night. His head was hot, and he was tingling. The only thing he wanted to do was to sleep, to separate what he had seen himself from the talk that had been washing in confused waves over him.

'It's been quite a day,' sighed Willis, contemplating the small disc of brandy that remained suspended in his balloon. 'I think all this weather has finally got to us, don't you?'

Rosemary swept the shawl over her shoulder, sending out a slipstream of perfume. 'Dear Geoffrey,' she said, 'is there something wrong? Do tell me. Now they've disappeared off to bed.'

She was moving around the perimeter of the drawing-room, turning off the lights one by one.

'That woman,' he told her, his voice rough from tobacco, 'that Miss Mackenzie. I'm afraid she's not at all well.'

'Her heart?' asked Rosemary. 'Is that it?'

He closed his eyes slowly. 'I just don't know. Her body — her arms especially. I've never seen anything like it. They were covered in patches, lesions, if you will. It just looked as if she had been burned.'

'But that's not possible, surely?'

'No. No. They weren't burns. Definitely not. But she was in a bad way, poor old stick. I rather wish I hadn't gone.'

'Poor you,' murmured Rosemary Cooper, 'what a busman's holiday you have had.'

XVII

The long stalk of kelp was thicker than his wrist, frosted with salt and sand, its point shattered where the currents had threshed it adrift from the floor of the sea. He picked it up from the rock-face and hurled it down on to the beach, then leapt after it, one arm thrust aloft, like a marauder storming a deck. He landed and crouched, scanning from left to right, around the dripping angles of the headland where the water gargled in amongst the gullies.

He would fire it, he would set the whole island to the torch. With the new threshold of the sky high above him, the sun again bright but seemingly washed clean, James hurtled off along the sand, leaping into the air, a pirate flailing his arms, and laughing.

The tide was not yet half-way in, slow yards from the ragged line of flotsam that had been flung up along the beach where the sunken sea looked as if it could never reach. Tins, netting, sacks, a shoe, shards of wood lay scattered as after an explosion, bandaged with dried foam. There were glistening hanks of submarine weed, tough and laminated like coils of gigantic pasta through which starlings hopped and heckled in search of sea-worms.

It might be the last chance he had to stand on his beach for a year, an almost unimaginable length of time. James could never quite picture the curve of it, for the calendar in his mind was always shifting its proportions – sometimes he saw it from a point around June, which seemed early on, though it was already half-way through. For some reason, the later months in a year looked bigger and longer; it was the same with the ribbon of numbers he held in his mind, from one to a hundred. The lower ones up to twenty seemed so much more nearby, the spaces between them wider, while the later ones – thirty, forty, fifty – had somehow all bunched up next to one another like a concertina, squashing away into a straight but indistinct line.

He unbuckled his sandals and stuffed his soggy socks into a trouser pocket. Despite the keen strength of the breeze the air was warm, the grey water looking muscular and strong away to the bold horizon. He ploughed his toes once more into the sand and stood for a moment as they were gradually covered by the tingling mass.

'Watch me disappear!' he shouted, the brisk air snatching his words and dashing off over the dunes. He looked at the sea blinking like a crowd in the sun.

He ran on. 'Watch me disappear,' he cried happily as he collided with the sudden cushions of the wind. When he reached the dunes he was still not out of breath and he scaled their slope without stopping, grabbed for support at the spiky grass, and stood proudly on the top, the crow's-nest, before collapsing with a slow roll sideways into his secret place.

A squadron of gannets passed overhead on its way to the morning's fishing. He watched the birds with their huge craning necks, and tried to judge the distance they were away from him. Once you were dealing with the air, it was almost impossible. James closed his eyes, one arm across his chest.

'Bareleg Benson,' he rehearsed to himself dramatically, 'the Terror of the Isles, was finally cut down on this spot, and his body burned by the enemy on top of the last tree left on the island.' The wind and the beat of the waters sounded distantly through the sand at his ears. 'But he carried the secret of his hidden treasure to the grave.'

For several minutes he lay there, the soft sand settling under him like a mould. Where would he be in a year's time, he wondered – at another school, another place where the familiar things that he knew, even if he did not particularly like them, would be gone. And he would be a different person, too; when you looked back on what had happened only the day before, it was someone slightly different it had all happened to. He cupped some sand and felt it dispersed by the wind, his eyelids very slightly apart.

When he reached the estuary, even his expectations had not prepared him for how much it was changed since he had stood there with Alec and watched the last light go from the shrunken stream. The little river was now swollen and quick, billowing its water out into the sea with a force that kept the brown sediment distinct for many yards before it fanned away and was absorbed into the long miles of the ocean.

There had been a bristling presence of fins thronging the area before, but now there was nothing to break the surface. With the tide low, it looked as if the sea in that bay must be gaunt and empty, having served its purpose and sunk back into old age. The breeze whirled through the iris leaves in their solitary bed like the brushing of wings against a pane.

The river itself now looked very deep. It ran smoothly over its submerged rocks with scarcely a sound. On the far side where the sand made a last crescent beach before the promontory escalated once again, James could see three gulls tugging at something dark and heavy-looking. They were stalking around it, twisting their heads, pulling and beating their wings as they wrenched pieces off it with their yellow beaks.

From where he stood it looked like a drowned dog. He decided to wade across, if he could, and take a closer look; his feet were already wet, and anyway he would have to change his trousers before lunch. James stepped gingerly into the water, and his feet disappeared from sight even in the darkness of the shallows. The bottom felt cold as a blade, and it was hard and clean, not the greasy rock it had been before the storm.

He was not even a third of the way across when his left foot slipped on a shifting stone, and he went over backwards. The water was not deep, but his right hand jerked out instinctively for support and he grazed several fingers. When he stood up, both pockets began spewing water, and the worsted was clinging to his legs like bark. There was nothing to lose now, so he plunged his way forward, and tried to squeeze himself a little drier on the opposite bank, though doing so just made him feel more clammy and cold.

As he emerged from the water, the birds cartwheeled away from their quarry a short distance, with cries like the squeaking of chalk against a blackboard. They stood on a rock, their heads angling mechanically at him.

It was not until he got quite close that he caught the sweetish, thin, rather antiseptic smell. The boy could not place it at all, nor could he recognise the hairy bundle the birds had been attacking. It was obviously dead: there were small, slivering worms weaving over the blanched skin, but he could not identify the mass as it lay there, so he turned it quickly over with his foot.

There was a sighing sound as it sank on to its back, and he found himself staring down into the face of a monkey.

He stepped back at once, appalled by what he saw, unable to comprehend exactly what it was. Certainly, it resembled a monkey, although one half of the skull was missing, or had been eaten away, whether by the sea or by birds he could not tell, and what remained of the face was shrivelled and bleached. The eyes had long since gone, and the skin around the head was blistered and coming away in soft little shreds. The two rows of yellow teeth seemed intact.

The boy leaned over and inspected it with a mixture of fascination and disgust. Whatever it was, whatever it had been, the creature was ugly and yet, in this setting, a peculiarity that suddenly had no reference to the rest of the shoreline. It had evidently been in the sea for quite a long time, and the brine had pickled it so that it had neither the reek nor the texture of putrefaction. It was saturated, but when he prodded it, it felt quite firm, though a small gush of liquid oozed from its chest on to his finger.

Both legs the were missing and there was no sign of a tail, but two sets of claws were curled stiffly up against the neck, as if bunched for the chin to lean upon. The hair had been torn away in irregular patches, and the exposed skin was blotchy as if mottled with some kind of rash; but the curious thing was that there seemed to be a sort of collar or strap around the disintegrating neck, a rusted buckle embedded in what remained of the sinew.

James had a sudden picture of this animal as some sailor's pet, lost overboard and drowned; thrown, maybe. It was still very difficult to see how it had got there at all, but it was quite a precious discovery, and he wanted someone else to inspect it.

It was not until late in the afternoon, when the men had returned from the loch and were eating their tea, that he managed to see Alec on his own. He was tidying the tackle-room and stripping the lines off the reels, to dry overnight.

'I hope I'm not bothering you,' said the boy tentatively. Alec had behaved so confusingly the last time he had tried to get through to him. James asked him about the day's sport, and whether there was any news of his aunt, and received brief, rather formal replies.

'Well, could I go and visit her, do you think?'

The man's head jerked up with an expression of alarm. 'No,' he said emphatically and then looked down again, shifting a little on his feet. 'No, Master James. I wouldn't be troubling yourself. She's fast on the mend, that one.'

'Why do you call me that? Is something wrong, Alec?'

The man looked furtively towards the door. 'It's Grant,' he hissed. 'Told me I must, and show respect. And if I'm not doing exactly as he says, then I'm out at the end of the year, boy, when he's had his words with the laird.'

'I'm sorry,' James told him. 'I didn't realise what had happened.'

'Oh, aye,' he went on in a hoarse whisper, 'and that's the thing of it now, Seumas, for he has me where he's wanting me. But that surely won't go on for ever. That bastard can be thinking what he will, in the mean time.'

The boy nodded, and there was a pause. 'Alec,' he said, 'there's something funny down by the estuary. I saw it this morning, on the shore. It looks like a dead monkey.'

There was a loud laugh from Alec, which surprised the boy, since it had seemed as if his sunken, defensive mood was never going to change. 'A monkey now, is it?' he asked, leaning forward on the table and shaking his head. 'What in heaven's name will you ever be dreaming up next, Seumas *ban*? A monkey. Now that's a thing I never heard of yet in this island.' He started rubbing his wiry eyebrows with the heel of his wrist. 'And was it,' he went on, 'from a circus that it came, are you thinking, or was it a native of these parts? There's plenty boys from Lewis could be mistaken for wee apes, even in daylight there's no doubt about it. Aye. If it was wearing the tweeds of a *Leodhasach* then a monkey it was for certain.'

James was so pleased to see this old spirit reviving in Alec that he didn't mind his discovery being the occasion of a joke. He giggled and smiled along with the man, happy that the droll island humour had resurfaced again between them.

'Can you come with me and have a look? It was quite interesting, but there were bits missing. I'm not really sure. Would you be allowed to?'

Alec came round the table at him and grabbed him by the shoulders. 'There's nobody here says whether Alec Campbell may, or may not, do a thing when he has a mind to it, big fellow. Are you forgetting that already then?' He picked up his stick from the table, slung the long coat over one shoulder and steered the boy by the small of the back towards the open door. 'Take us to yon monkey,' he ordered, 'and we'll be telling if he's a McIver or maybe even a Grant!'

The tide was almost at its full, the curd of the surf curving high along the sands. Alec walked very slowly, his breathing loud after only a few minutes, but his face showed the determination to reach his objective once his mind was made up.

'Is she really all right?' asked James carefully. 'Miss Mackenzie, I mean. I was very sorry to hear about her.' He had understood from the man's reaction that it was not a matter he wanted to discuss, but the boy was concerned; perhaps she had forbidden him to visit for some reason, she might even be dying. It didn't quite make sense.

'And didn't I tell you just now,' came the reply, its attempt to sound level being broken by his struggle in breathing, 'she'll be righter than rain once she's rested. Do they never teach you listening at that school of yours, boy?'

'So it's nothing terribly serious?'

Alec stopped, more to catch his breath than to create an effect. His mouth was closed and his nostrils flared as he heaved to control the oxygen. 'She took fright,' he said, 'from a fall she had. Thought it was the stroke come at last, with her speech not over easy just after, from the shock of it. Sure, she'll be up and about tomorrow, with my Christina there to help her, so she will.'

He felt relieved at this news. 'Maybe I could see her then. I'd like just to say goodbye before we go home. Would that be all right?'

'We'd have to see,' Alec told him, 'and I'm thinking she'd no want to miss you. But it's not for us to decide – there's Doctor Graham in charge of her now, and a fine doctor he is, too, if he is from Aberdeen. I had my Auntie Rachel up to the hospital to see him this morning, for the tests, and he was saying she'd to rest herself and stay in her bed. But we'll see yet.'

He limped on, his mouth set in a slight smile as he fought the pain of his movements.

James heard himself speak as if he were listening to someone else asking the question. 'What does it mean, Second Sight?' He had walked slowly on for several paces before he realised Alec had stopped behind him, and was staring in his direction, one hand thrust like a comb into his hair.

'Seumas Benson,' he said deliberately, frowning at the boy.
'Did you ever hear told the time the Devil took young
Ruaraidh the cobbler out on a moonlit night to the Cave of
the Seven Harps? No? Well, I'm telling you now, it's said he
did it only because Ruaraidh was a hunchback, and the old
one wanted to laugh at his walking. And is it that you've
been doing,' he continued, his features breaking into a smile,
'getting a poor man such as myself to come following you
along a beach of sand to be asked such a question about the
Two Sights while we look for a monkey?'

He made his halting way up to the boy, who stood pale
and confused on the sand. '*An da shealladh* now, is it? The
Two Sights you'd be trying me with?' He clasped James
firmly on the elbow. 'If you're wanting to pull the leg of a
person, you've chosen your wrong man, Seumas, for it's lame
enough I am already.'

'But somebody told my father she had Second Sight,' he
repeated seriously. 'And no one goes to see her, and she lay
there on her own.' He had a vague idea of what they had
been referring to, but now it seemed important that he knew.

'Seumas *ban*, Seumas *ban*. I'm knowing full well who's been
saying these things, but it's never the truth. There's scarce a
day goes by when my auntie doesn't receive a visitor, and it
was Christina herself found her the very next morning, when
she went with her books from the travelling library.' Alec
shook his elbow reassuringly. 'And she needs the large print,
do you see, for she's the cataracts that bad. Never be minding
any of your Second Sight – she couldna see the sun in the sky
without her spectacles, that one!'

'But what does it mean?' His fists were clenched by his
side, he was sure there was something missing.

'It's all for the tourists,' said Alec, 'to bring them up to the
misty islands. Believe me, it's an invention that's been going
for years, the only thing that's known about us apart from
the tweeds and the whisky. And what's the harm in it? None
at all. I never in my life met a person could look into the

middle of next week except when there was the drink taken, and we'd believe anything at all that was said.'

They walked on together, aware that the business was not yet finished. 'If it's the mysteries of this island you're interested in,' began Alec slowly, 'you'd be better by far considering the wonder of it that there's scarce a fishing-boat put out by our boys from one summer to the next, where there used to be hundreds. If I had the Sight,' he concluded, 'then maybe I could tell you what all that will do for us in the end.'

When they reached the mouth of the river it was clear they would not even have to worry about how to wade across; the carcass had gone. The part of the shore where James remembered it lying was covered in water, and there was no sign of anything floating nearby. Suddenly, he was more disappointed than he could understand.

'It was there,' he said miserably, remembering their fruitless searching for the sheep. 'But it's gone.'

'So it has indeed.' The man leaned heavily on his stick, and surveyed the surface of the estuary. 'Well, what could have been the use of it anyway, except to have seen it and told the tale? It's better gone, Seumas. The sea is a great cleanser.'

They turned and made their way back along the beach. James began to trudge gloomily, his hands thrust into his pockets; his fingers closed around something hard, which he tugged out sideways, craning awkwardly as he did so. The lining of the pocket emerged like a stomach, dislodging its contents – two postage stamps, a stub of pencil, a bull's-eye matted with fluff, and the bloodstone he had picked out of the rock.

'Here,' he said, offering it on his palm. 'I want you to have it.'

The man lifted his hand, then hesitated.

'You keep it,' insisted James, 'it's for you.'

Alec picked it gently up between his finger and thumb and, turning away toward the sea, he held it to his eye.

. . . . .

'Hang on a moment, young fellow,' said Willis with a look of extreme bewilderment, 'What did you say it was? Just tell us again.'

'A monkey,' replied James. 'I'm pretty sure it was a dead monkey. That's what it looked like.'

Bobby Paton squinted into his brandy. 'That seems unlikely, to say the least.'

'It could have been almost anything, really,' concluded Willis, 'an otter, a cat, even a baby seal. Everything tends to look rather the same after it's been in the water for any period of time. And I know: I've seen a fair share of drowned bodies in my time.'

'And the Gulf Stream, what about that?' added Cooper. 'Comes up this way, doesn't it? Keeps everything warm in winter. I know a chap on Mull – Freddy Maitland, you know – grows pineapples for a hobby. Says he find coconuts and such things washed up in his bay; come all the way from the Caribbean.'

'Coconuts float almost indefinitely,' said Paton with an air of authority, 'whereas monkeys, on the whole, do not.'

Alice looked at him contemptuously. 'I had a friend at school who discovered the tail of a rat in her pork pie,' she told him. 'It is sometimes difficult to explain where everything comes from.'

'You have an extraordinary passion for irrelevancies, do you know that?'

Geoffrey Willis was fiddling his fingers around inside his pouch of tobacco. 'But it's interesting as a hypothesis, isn't it,' he mused, 'because evidently there was something unusual there that young James stumbled across, and that's one of the things about the sea, I've always thought: there's probably hundreds of creatures swimming about that we've never clapped eyes on. That chappie, the South African. Dredged up a fish, aren't I right, earlier this year – something like thirty million years old, a living fossil? Makes you wonder.' He began to concentrate on puffing his smoke. 'Does me, any rate.'

'No need to blind us with science, Geoffrey. Fossilised fish!'

'Oh, come on Bobby. You read about it, same as I did. Fair's fair. What was it called? I forget.'

Alice leaned forward. 'Coelacanth,' she told them, 'they've called it a coelacanth.'

'It wasn't any fish,' James said loudly, angry at the way they were making fun of what he had told them about his discovery. 'Why don't you believe it?' He was aware of the men staring at him in sudden disapproval. 'Well it's true.'

His father looked severe. 'Now then, young man. Steady on.'

It must have been some time early in the morning when he awoke, but he was not sure of the hour; it could almost have been some other day altogether. He felt as if his head had grown to the size of the entire room, and when he lay in the fizzing dark he was looking at the inside of his own skull. There was a pulsing sound he could not control, but whether from inside the room or his own head it was impossible to tell. It continued even when he held his breath.

His skull was a globe, the upper hemisphere planted with grasses and corn, with animals browsing it. James held his bed-clothes as the pillows seemed to spin, and then there came a fat, splitting sound, like rain smacking into a gutter. He shook his head, but it took a long time to clear. Somewhere up in the tangle above him were the caged birds of the wind hurtling among rafters.

XVIII

As he picked his way down the track towards the house and saw the air above her chimney rigged with smoke in the calm sunshine, James felt for the first time the coming sadness of leaving the island. It was this place with its close room, with its feeling of permanence, that he was going to miss and remember – not the more massive lodge, uncomfortable and out of place in its surroundings, where now the women were checking inventories and packing away their things.

The guns had mounted a final expedition that day to shoot some birds to take south for their friends, but he had not seen Alec in the morning; he was still not fit enough to take the hill. James had not been able to ask him about his aunt, but this afternoon was the last chance of visiting her, so he had decided to go even without permission. He wanted to say goodbye, and to thank her for all the times she had welcomed him into her home.

He had never been into the old black house that remained like a shuck behind the newer building. Just as he was passing it, though, he heard a faint hammering sound, irregular, as if someone were rummaging around in a drawer. His first thought was that it must be Christina, whom he knew was looking after the old woman, so he decided to have a word with her before arriving unannounced at Miss Mackenzie's house. James stood and called her name, and the noise stopped at once, but there was no reply.

It was not until he had already slid back the rough bolt that he realised there could not be anyone inside. At first he could see almost nothing: it was surprisingly small, as the stone walls were several feet thick, and the air was damp and heavy. There was a single, small window set low in the wall facing him, but it was grimy and let in little light. He could make out a central beam with blades and other tools hanging from it, and a clutter of boxes and tins. It smelled like the sort of place that would be thick with hanging cobwebs, so he stayed in the doorway until his eyes had properly adjusted to the gloom.

It seemed hardly believable that this had once been the house of an entire family; it was little better than a coal hole. The floor was of damp, compacted earth, and the whole interior was about the size of his bedroom at home. Once he could see better, James picked his way through the lumber, ducking under the beam, and went over to the window. The glass was strung across with spider-webs, like the delicate vessels of an eye, and he peered through it at the flat sea beyond. His face was almost touching the window before he realised that the glass was not dirty with age, but splashed with blood.

He had almost made it to the door when a whirling sound came exploding out of the rafters above him, and he threw himself down sideways on to a huge heap of netting, arms flailing around his head to protect himself. In a panic to reach the open air he ripped the arm of his duffel against a nail, and came spinning out on to the rough grass.

Only a few yards from the doorway there was a white bird lying awkwardly on the ground, one black webbed foot sticking out sideways. It was smaller than any gull he had seen, and from its longish, yellow beak there issued a thin stream of blood. The base of its neck, too, was smudged and pink where it had scrabbled against the window and spattered itself. James got to his feet and skirted it warily; the bird followed him with its gold-ringed eye, then heaved its wings and began to paddle jerkily over the ground like some clockwork toy. He ran for the house.

It was Christina who opened the door when he knocked. 'Well, Seumas, and it is you after all, when I was wondering at the commotion. But whatever have you been doing? With your fine coat torn open, and yourself as pale as milk. You'd best be coming in,' she beckoned, standing aside, 'for it looks as if your heart would be out of its shell.'

There was no sign of Miss Mackenzie in her kitchen. He stood by the table, feeling the thick pump of his heart, and explained why he had come. Christina said the woman was still resting, and he could see her briefly when she awoke, but in the meanwhile he should sit and take his tea.

'I got a bit of a fright,' James told her, once he was settled. 'I heard something in the hut, I thought it was you. But it was a bird. It must have been trapped somehow, and hurt itself. It gave me a real shock.'

She put down her cups suddenly, her lips thin and tight. 'That's it then,' she said, 'the bird in the house.'

'In the hut,' he repeated.

'In the black house.' She shook her head, looking stern. 'Well, it would be best not to tell her of that, with the poor state she's in. There's nothing can be done.'

'Why?'

Christina flapped her hands dismissively. 'Ach, no reason at all; but she's no very easy in herself, and there's no sense in alarming her. With you having had the fright on it, that's all now.' She started to butter the bread stiffly, as if concentrating.

'Is Miss Mackenzie better now?'

'You can see her once she's woken,' she said again, 'but she's not to get excited at all. The doctor's orders. He wanted her in the hospital, but she'd no be moved from here. She's nothing too well, the *cailleach*, but I'd no idea. She was thinking she heard the dead-drop, but I was telling her no. I'd no idea. No idea it was that bad.'

And later, when he entered the small room, hot with the smell of sickness, James could not disguise how startled he was at the way the old woman had changed. The skin of her face, which had been a weathered craquelure of fine lines like the veins in a current, was now deeply scored and there were several dull blotches upon it, and others up the broad arms that lay parallel along the fringes of the woven blankets.

'Miss Mackenzie?' he said in a soft voice. It was not clear whether she was properly awake, for her eyes were almost closed. 'I'm sorry you're not feeling too well. I've come to say goodbye.'

He realised he should have brought her something; when you visited sick people you gave them fruit or flowers.

When she spoke, her voice had thinned, had lost its steady rhythm. The left side of her mouth twisted downwards slightly, making certain words difficult to hear. 'You've come then, Seumas. Sit you down, if there's any place. I'm glad.'

'You've to take a warm drink, Raonaid, once I've fetched it in,' said Christina, leaving them alone.

'She worries,' the woman told him, 'but she's a good provider, that one. How is the sea?'

James was not at all sure what she meant. 'Very nice,' he assured her, 'it's quite calm. It's a lovely day.'

'Peace in the mouth of the beast, aye. With a storm vanished, that is the way. *Gair na mara*; the sea will be in her laughter now.' She opened her eyes at him, and he saw that they alone were unchanged, a sharp, still blue. 'It's a long journey you have before you, I'm thinking. Blessings upon it, and upon a friend.'

He looked at his feet, embarrassed by this compliment. There was a pause, and then her voice came again, but now with more of its usual strength.

'You have seen something, Seumas.'

'What?'

'What is it you have seen?'

He blushed immediately. 'Nothing,' he replied.

Miss Mackenzie began slowly to worm her way up into a sitting position, clutching at the sheet behind her head. 'I am old,' she said, 'and the vision is not so clear. But there is a thing you have to tell me.'

'No honestly.' He peered hopefully through the half-open

door, his face burning; but Christina was still busy at the far end of the kitchen.

Her voice was now powerful but low. 'You have seen the bird. I know this. Where?'

His tongue seemed to contract drily, and he could say nothing. He found himself locked in her gaze, and then heard his voice, as if from a distance, saying, 'In the black house.'

At the keening wail that the woman let out, Christina came hurrying back into the little room. She went straight to the bedside, and started to pull the shivering old woman back down between the sheets, a hand on each shoulder. 'Whatever is it?' she demanded of James. 'What have you said?'

'I couldn't help it; I'm sorry.'

'*Raonaid, Raonaid – de tha thu deanamh? Tha sin gu leor,*' said the younger woman urgently.

'You must listen,' cried Rachel Mackenzie in a high voice.

'No,' said Christina, 'nothing more, nothing more.'

'It is him has seen the bird, he must know now. *Cairistiona!* The bird, and the sun, and fire on my arm, he has seen them all. He should know the meanings.' She gestured Christina away from the bed, and she complied, slowly withdrawing, her head shaking, as far as the bare little dresser.

Miss Mackenzie's voice began to ring in the air. Her eyes were open extraordinarily wide, the lids appearing to curl outwards. 'There was once born in that house a girl child, and I was the mother of her,' she cried. 'A daughter I had, when I returned to this place from the south of England many years, many years ago. Beautiful she was to me, but Bride would not hear me and she was taken by the scourge; at three weeks old she was taken, and here have I stayed since that day, but she lies now in that part of the church yard where no one will trouble her more. And the white bird was seen in those days.'

James sat frozen with incomprehension at the foot of the bed. He could hear Christina Campbell behind him, crying through the mask of her fingers.

'There is no receiving but the world must give back,' continued the old woman, pointing at the wall, 'and the sign of it will be seen, though it has not yet come. My father it was knew the tale; and it is remembered. At a time when the land was still covered with trees, a widow there was out on the shore by this very point, gathering shellfish and weed for her meal. And she heard from a fold in the rocks the skoyling sound of an infant crying, and she went to look, and she found instead a pup of a seal it was making that very noise.'

She uttered another wail, like that of a seabird or a small child. The boy watched her, transfixed. It was obvious to him that she had gone mad in her illness.

'And what she did was to gather him up, and carried him back to her house where she lived alone, and there she brought him up as a human boy so that in time he no longer had about him the bitter smell of the sea, but he began to change. The smell of him was that of the honey that every child in the island will have, and he lived in her house. And when he was eight years of age, in a dark creek to the north of here, he saw the White Bird.'

Her body was now rigid, and the shakings had ceased. The blood had come into her face, obliterating the marks on her skin, making her look much younger.

'The White Bird will be swan and eagle both, and when the moon grows and a tide is on the flow he takes the appearance of a bright-eyed man, and moves among us all. It will be a happy year indeed: the struggling soldier shall know no defeat, and the wounded one will see a white woman who will heal him.' Her taut voice snapped into a series of coughs, her eyes rolled, and she sagged on to the pillows.

'You should go,' Christina told him, moving briskly to the bed. 'I will have the doctor brought. But you should be going.'

The boy stood up at once, and pushed open the bedroom door. He wanted to get out of the house and to breathe some fresh air on his own. There was nothing else he could say.

'*Fuirich mionaid,* Seumas *ban* – wait here on me one minute,' she asked, her voice exhausted. He went over to the bed, anxious and reluctant. Miss Mackenzie reached up and pulled his head gently down towards her, and kissed him on the brow. Her lips felt as hard as bark.

'A blessing on you,' she said. '*Mo chubhrachan.*'

He escaped into the early light of the evening, Christina standing concerned in the doorway. As he passed the old house he looked around for the wounded bird, but instinctively he knew that it would be nowhere to be seen.

. . . . .

He stood on the rear deck and watched the island recede. It was not long before it seemed to be one mass of grey rock, the houses and the patches of cultivation dissolved into their surroundings, the lines of the land rising, ragged and clear, as they had been for three thousand million years.

Once away from the forked arms of the long harbour, the wind came hard and cold from the south. James pushed his fists into the pockets of his coat, the sleeve still scarred with its white tear. His fingers played with the soft skin of the pencil-case that Alec had given him that morning as they shook hands in a formal goodbye, and the cartons of game were loaded into the cars, and the long journey south began.

Somewhere beyond him, there on the other side of the great hills, was the loch where he had caught his fish, and the shuttered lodge, the old woman he had met, and the secret hollow behind the dunes. They were draining away out of him, settling back into their proper places, as if they had never been his.

'Time for luncheon,' announced his father, rubbing his hands. 'Down we go. No point in getting frozen. Come on.'

They descended into the noisy interior of the ship.

His father turned and looked at him. 'And do take off that ridiculous hat.'

XIX

As far as he could tell, Mrs Cassell only made her toffee two days before the start of each school term. Its otherwise comforting, burnt smell that permeated the kitchen end of their house was the start of a countdown through a familiar routine which ended at the main line station as the school train from London drew up steaming in the half light. In a curious way, those last two days always seemed to pass most slowly, and it was something of a relief to snap down the handle of the carriage and join the loud faction of the other gabbling boys.

These last days filled him with an empty, rather disembodied feeling as if he did not belong in his home. A vague dread tingled in his stomach each time he passed the open door of the spare room and glimpsed, inside, the waiting trunk and the orderly ranks of regulation clothes serried upon the cover of the bed – clothes that he had not seen for two months; lace-up brown shoes with crêpe rubber soles, football shirts folded and stacked like hateful hanks of dough, the two vee-necked pullovers in the uniform russet and green.

But this time the feeling of limbo was even greater, for weeks away on the island had made the crowded Surrey landscape look strange, with its bulging barriers of rhododendrons, the bent laburnum with its dark pods – damp trees everywhere breaking the skyline. The garden bristled with crisping hydrangeas and solemn goldenrod, the pond was silky and green, the ground dotted with brown little birds, the air full of bonfire smoke and the noises of invisible machinery. From time to time the island floated through his mind, but it was distant and small and he could not yet pull it in closely; it had nothing to do with the reality of the approaching term.

And when the Thursday afternoon finally arrived it was much the same as ever, as he watched the instrument panel on his father's dashboard indicate the distance left between his home and the place where he must join the rest of the school. The term began with the moment you boarded the train; the first time he had done this he had been delivered to the station dressed in his grey Sunday suit, for his mother had ignored the school regulations and insisted that a proper gentleman travelled in his smartest clothes, but the rest of the boys were wearing the school uniform. On the platform, his mother had held him, damp faced, and smoothed his hair while several boys leaned out of the carriage windows, frowning as she clutched him. Critchley, a boy in the third form, had told James he would be beaten for breaking the rules, and he had spent half an hour in the locked lavatory, arms pressed against his dribbling eyes.

'Well, I think you had a good holiday at any rate,' his father told him as the Healey swung into the station car-park. 'Put colour in your cheeks, ready for the fray. Shall we go again next year – what do you say?'

James said yes, of course. He shook hands with his father, and thanked him for the pound note he was tipped. The train had already drawn into the station, and he could imagine them staring out at him.

Richard Benson patted his son on the shoulder. 'Important year coming up for you, remember. Got to win that scholarship in the summer. Stay up in front, make me proud.'

'Yes,' he said. 'Yes. I'll try.' James tugged open the door and waded into the swell of talk and laughter.

.   .   .   .   .

He had been back at Slatebrook less than a week when he began without warning to get little attacks of shivering; his urine came out burningly, cloudy and thick, and at times his legs felt as if they were made of cotton-wool. James went to see Miss Reynolds, the head-matron, and she gave him some cod-liver oil. A few days later his legs gave way completely as he was climbing out of a hot bath, and he collapsed on to the linoleum floor; Miss Reynolds tucked him up in the sickroom, and made him a drink of warm milk. He went into a deep but fitful sleep.

It was one of those dreams where you believe you can stop what is happening whenever you want. He was standing in a wood, a vague moonlit place with the sound of running water somewhere nearby: he couldn't see it, and it was difficult to turn his head, but he wanted to reach out and plunge his hands into it. There was somebody singing – a woman, but he couldn't see her either. He tried to move forward, but his legs wouldn't work, and when he looked down he saw that he was naked, and his body was covered in coarse hair.

James awoke with a thick pain deep down in his chest. The matron was standing over his bed, holding one wrist in her hand.

'How are we feeling, Benson?' she asked.

He tried to reply, but his mouth was sticky and he could not say the words. He was aware of a warm patch under his pyjamas, and a sweet smell rising from the cocoon of his sheets.

'Lie still,' she said, and slipped the bulb of her thermometer under his tongue. 'We'll soon have you cleared up.'

It was six o'clock in the morning, and his temperature read 104 degrees. For an hour he lay in the dim light, each breath coming hard like sucking in a lungful of feathers. He was too hot to feel frightened, and when the school doctor arrived and took a sample of saliva, the boy did not notice that the swab was tinged with blood.

This time he was underwater, with a dull roaring noise in his ears. There were boulders moving slowly, and piles of quivering raw meat, and the water was warm. Then he was lying on a long black rock in the open air; the sun was hot and low over the sea, but whether it was rising or setting he could not tell. At one stage he thought he saw his father in the distance, and then his mother, but after that he no longer recognised what he saw.

. . . . .

Richard Benson went straight to the hospital as soon as he heard. He had to wear a paper mask before he could enter the boy's room, and once he was in he stayed close to the door and did not approach the bed. James's head lay still in the cleft of the swollen pillows, and his eyes were closed. They were feeding him oxygen through a face-mask, and the room felt terribly cold.

'My name is Franklin,' said a man in white from behind his surgical mask. 'Perhaps we could have a word? I've just got down from London.'

'What is it?' Benson demanded. 'What the hell is happening?' He kept his voice low, but the urgency remained.

'Not sure, just at present. We're still running tests,' replied Franklin, raising his clipboard. 'But whatever it is, your son has a very interesting condition, Mr Benson.'

'How serious is it?'

'Well, he's running a high fever. Very high. We're trying to bring that down, of course, and in itself it shouldn't be dangerous, unless there are complications.'

Benson stared at him severely. 'Such as?' He was beginning to feel frightened.

'There's some sort of bacterial infection here, seems rather virulent, like a form of pneumonia. Never come across it before. Chest X-rays show a certain discharge in the region of the lungs, pleurisy, you understand, but we've drugs for that. And he's taking the oxygen. But there's also the poly-morphs – blood test shows they're up, and I'd like to see that situation reversed. Just give us time. We've all hands on deck.'

'I'm sorry. What are you saying?'

205

'The white cell count. It's on the high side. That's what we're working on.'

Richard Benson sat down in a chair, his back not touching it. He looked across at the face of his son as they unstrapped the mask, and the lips were visibly blue. It was the first time for years that he realised he was helpless.

When the boy opened his eyes he saw nothing of this. There were red rocks, and water licking around them, a low sky streaked with colour. He could hear the voices washing over him from far away, shaken and distant as if through the wind. His body trembled in the heat of the bed, as the cells spiralled through him, a white bird whirling in the blood.

As his father looked at him, he felt something buckle slowly inside, like a column of paper burning, curling into ash. 'Why don't you come,' he heard a nurse say, 'and I'll fix you some nice tea.'

James lay in his flowing heat. Later that evening, his system burst like a bore-tide, and he died.

．　．　．　．　．

It was too early for snow, but still it sifted down like leaves on to the stiffened sand. Beyond, the light was dancing, yellow and red and blue, shaking its spectral spears, the ribbons unravelling high above the water, and brighter than had ever been seen.

Rachel Mackenzie had her chair turned toward the window, and though she could not speak her eyes followed the quick runners as they pulsed through the autumn sky. Alec sat by her side, the blood-stone in his palm, as they witnessed the spectacle.

'*Fuil siochaire*,' he said, 'the blood of the dancers.'

Next morning, he walked to the estuary where the broad stream still thrust out into the bay. He felt his way among the crevasses and found a place where he could drop the stone into a small cup worn by the sea, and then he went to the iris bed and tore away some of the brittle leaves.

And out it went, the little boat, twirling and bobbing over the current, until he could no longer see it against the dark skin of the water.